STAR TREK®
INSURRECTION™

STAR TREK®
INSURRECTION™

A Novel by J. M. Dillard
Based on STAR TREK: INSURRECTION
Story by Rick Berman & Michael Piller
Screenplay by Michael Piller

POCKET BOOKS
New York   London   Toronto   Sydney   Tokyo   Singapore

POCKET BOOKS, a division of Simon & Schuster Inc.
1230 Avenue of the Americas, New York, NY 10020

A VIACOM COMPANY

STAR TREK is a Registered Trademark of Paramount Pictures.

This book is published by Pocket Books, a division of Simon & Schuster Inc., under exclusive license from Paramount Pictures.

ISBN: 0-671-02447-7

To Jack Benny, wherever you are

STAR TREK®
INSURRECTION™

ONE

☆

The morning of what would become the Day of Lightning began like all other spring days: cool first, then warmed by the rising sun. Anij paused in her walking to gaze up at the mountains, stark and serene against a cloudless sky. Timeless they were, as timeless as the sunlight, warm upon her homespun-clad shoulders; as timeless as the morning, or the cool air moving through her lungs, or her consciousness itself. She had walked this particular path into town every day for the past—how many mornings? *Always,* she told herself, *forever;* for she did not care to remember the Time before this one. Forever the Ba'ku had lived here, or so it seemed; forever they had enjoyed the wealth of the fertile valley. And every day, regardless

1

of season, it was the same: she set upon her way and saw the same sights—the valley lush and verdant, fragrant with wildflowers and herbs, the tilled crops healthy in the dark, eternally fruitful soil; the imposing backdrop of mountains sometimes taupe, sometimes rose, sometimes blue or mauve, everchanging with the play of the light. Even when the rains came, they were gentle: perfect, simply perfect, never enough to keep her inside.

And every morning, the intense beauty of her world startled her afresh and filled her with joy.

Anij glanced up at the sound of a bleat: upon the lower, greener hillsides, shaggy pack animals grazed, a few of them glancing up at the shouts of children playing on a nearby farm. She followed the animals' curious gazes to a group of children clearly on the prowl for something hidden. Two of the boys were scanning the hay-strewn troughs between mounds of tender young plants—careful, of course, not to trample the all-important crops. Meantime, a mixed trio ran giggling through the nearby orchard.

Anij smiled absently at them—she knew them by name, of course, and their parents—and resumed her customary stroll as she watched them. Suddenly, a golden head popped out from a haystack, and glanced about, searching for pursuers.

"There he is!" one of the girls bellowed, and Anij's faint smile turned to a wide grin as small shoulders,

elbows, knees, and finally, an entire body, erupted from the haystack in a flurry of airborne straw. This was her youngest friend, the twelve-year-old Artim. His mother Barel had been a dear friend, too, and upon her tragic early passing immediately after the boy's birth, Anij came to serve as a foster aunt. Artim had proven such a delight—wise beyond his years, with his mother's sweet disposition—that Anij judged the child to be the true benefactor in the relationship.

Laughing to the point of breathlessness, Artim scrambled past the reach of his pursuers and up the trail that led into the rocky foothills, leaving a shower of pebbles in his wake. Anij watched as the others followed him, crying out in happy indignation at his escape, while she continued her journey. It would lead her on a slowly upward-winding trail into the village, where her path would intersect that of the children as they emerged from their steeper, more challenging route.

Sojef, Artim's father, would be waiting there; Sojef, straight and solemn, always and forever with a question in his eyes.

And Anij, with the same answer in hers: *Not yet, not yet* . . .

She had always thought her answer was based on purely solid reasoning: that she was still young, and

Sojef, too; that there was still time for such commitments, for children. True, he was a good man—leader of the entire Ba'ku community, six hundred now, and growing slowly again after so many were lost during the Time of Sorrows. She knew, also, from the now-departed Barel, that Sojef had been the most devoted of husbands, the gentlest of lovers.

A year after Barel's death, on his son's first birthday, Sojef had professed his love to Anij. Had asked her to commit to a permanent partnership. *Forever,* he had said.

Forever, Anij knew, was a very, very long time. Even so, she did not say no; at the same time, she did not say yes. *I don't know. Give me time, Sojef. Give me time . . .*

Time to accept that she would wed not out of passion, but friendship.

Sojef had given her time, of course; he was Ba'ku, too mature and intelligent to let something as foolish as his emotions cloud his judgment. And so, he and Artim remained her friends, visiting daily; it was understood in the village that perhaps someday, they would announce a formal commitment.

Anij drank in a long breath of cool morning air as she rounded a sharp curve in the path; the mountain that had blocked her view gave way suddenly to reveal the village square, encircled by the blooms of spring in dazzling shades of yellow, fuchsia, blue-violet. No matter how many times she saw that particular view, she always experienced pleasure.

How many springs had she experienced? Many, so many, and while she had always been aesthetically moved by the season's heady beauty, she had always reacted with wisdom and restraint. Only the youngest, most spoiled children indulged their emotions freely.

This spring was different; or perhaps it was she, Anij, who had somehow changed, grown tired of denying her feelings in favor of responsibility. The night before, she had dreamed a foolish dream: that she was free of all commitments, that she flew like a bird from the village and found her heart's desire in an offlander, a stranger whose face she could not clearly see, but whose strong arms held her firmly, whose whisper evoked in her an intensity of physical craving and emotion she had never before experienced.

She had wakened with a cry of disappointment at finding herself in her own bed, alone; even now, gazing upon the village nestled against mountains, sky, and quicksilver river, she felt a pang of yearning.

It followed her across the wildflower-filled meadow, past the pond into the village square, as she reasoned with it silently:

You are a fool, Anij, to think such thoughts. You know how craven, how amoral offlanders are; how could you even dream of loving one? Even dream of giving up this . . . ?

And the beauty and serenity of the valley soothed her, as it always did; by the time she greeted her first fellow villager, her smile was once again genuine. This was the place she belonged—had always belonged—and the joy of being here far outweighed any childish cravings for true passion.

People began milling into the square. Some of the first merchants to arrive had already set up their stalls in the shade of a large rockface, where the mountain met the village, and were displaying wares: homespun clothing, honey, medicinal herbs.

"Gen'a, good morning," she called, to a woman carrying pails of fresh milk for sale, and to her dark-haired husband, eldest of the Original Group: "Jat'ko, how are you?"

And there beside the market stall stood Sojef, dressed in plain homespun. Anij banished all thoughts of the hot-blooded offlander and looked upon Sojef with admiration: he was clothed like everyone else, yet a stranger could easily have identified him as a leader. Not because of any affectation or condescension in his manner or speech; Sojef's attitude was one of gentleness. But there was a strength behind it—a strength Anij had seen many times before, especially during the Time of Sorrows, when Sojef had taken responsibility for making the hardest decision of all.

She greeted him as she had every day for the past eleven years since his proposal: with a slight, complicitous smile, as if their agreement to become engaged someday were a secret unshared by the entire community. And he responded as he always did, with the same coconspirator's smile, the faint uncertainty in his eyes: *Do you love me yet, as I do you?*

And her unspoken answer: *Give me time . . .*

He nodded, ending the exchange, and turned his attention to others headed for market; he considered it his task to know each villager's challenges, hopes, needs . . . and dreams. Especially dreams.

Anij turned from him and headed for a produce stall, where a vendor was busily unloading the season's first *maj'ra* fruit for display. As Anij neared, the vendor stopped, produced a paring knife, and began to peel away a piece of the oblong fruit's white exterior to reveal the juicy, violet-colored flesh inside.

He sliced a dripping square of flesh off and passed it across the wooden stall to Anij, who took a grateful bite and winced with pleasure at the tartness. A sudden shudder passed through her—and with it, the unbidden, unsettling memory of the Time of Sorrows, the time when forever had almost stopped.

* * *

Within the rockface, behind the shields that rendered him invisible, Gallatin watched as the Ba'ku woman shuddered, then lifted her head and stared right at him.

Instinctively, his heart had begun to beat rapidly; impossibly, she had sensed him, perhaps recognized him—

No, he commanded himself. *See, she is just distracted, that's all, and staring into the distance . . . It's your own foolish guilt that has discovered you, Gal'na, not this woman.*

Still, he gazed down at his monitor to assure himself that the shields were in perfect working order. And of course, they were; she could no more see him than she could the uniformed Starfleet officer sitting beside Gallatin at the console, or the other researchers hidden in the blind—or, for that matter, the other isolation-suited researchers milling around the village square, rendered invisible by the force field that appeared to Gallatin as a bright red glow. One of them stood right beside her—close enough, at the moment, for her to touch should she suddenly start flailing her arms about.

But she would not, of course; she was a well-mannered Ba'ku, and like all her people, handsome. Particularly so, with her sun-bleached, close-cropped curls that framed delicate features . . .

. . . and those damnably ageless eyes. All the Ba'ku

had them, even the children, and for the umpteenth time that hour, Gallatin found himself struggling to master his hatred and envy.

Look at her, so casually wiping away the scarlet juice of the *maj'ra* fruit from her chin, from that soft, unmarked skin . . . Gallatin drew in a silent breath at its perfection. How radiant it was, how firm and unlined—while he and all his fellow Son'a were old, irretrievably old and bound soon for death, their genes so damaged that there was no hope of progeny, of sons and daughters to remind their parents of the beauty of youth. Many of the Son'a had already died. With none to replace them, they were an aged and dying race, destined for extinction within a decade, perhaps two. The mere sight of the Ba'ku offended him and filled him with longing.

Beside him at the console, a Starfleet lieutenant spoke into a companel. "Base to Ensign McCauley. Please report to area seven and assist the edaphology team."

"Acknowledged." Outside the duck blind, the glowing red observer next to the Ba'ku woman turned and moved away.

Gallatin paused to look at the lieutenant beside him—a middle-aged human female with wrinkles beginning to appear in the corners of her eyes, upon her brow. Any respectable Son'a would have taken prompt action to have them removed; yet humans and most other Federation races tolerated wrinkling gracefully, as if it were a natural event and not a disgusting side effect of mortality. Somehow, on them it seemed less hideous—but on a Son'a face, the slightest sag, the tiniest wrinkle, was a moral affront. Gallatin's own facial skin was pulled taut—*like a rotten melon about to split,* he thought in disgust. Between the daily facial surgeries and the genetic damage, he was just beginning to develop the chronic algal growth all Son'a dreaded, for it caused an unsightly dark-green mottling just beneath the skin. Over time, it disintegrated layers of delicate tissue from the inside out.

The sense of another warm body standing beside him drew his attention back to the present; he turned, and discovered another Starfleet officer, this one an ensign, proffering a computer padd. Gallatin took the padd and glanced cursorily at the readings, then at the ensign, a young human male of Caucasian variety, with skin an astounding fresh-scrubbed pink. How did the Son'a appear to him? Grotesque and decadent, most likely, with stretched, bloodless skin and sumptuous, ornate robes augmented by precious jewels. Not that Gallatin considered his own dress excessive; it was not the Son'a's fault that the entire known galaxy lacked any sense of style, or that Starfleet's designers adored the drab and unimaginative. A little gold-pressed latinum and onyx at the collar and shoulders, perhaps a large central ruby on the utility belt, just a few subtle changes here and there . . .

Decadent, Gallatin decided. *That is what they think we are: decadent, decrepit, and dying.* And at the sight of the ensign, and of the vibrant, unadorned beauty of the Ba'ku woman, he knew they were right.

He thrust the padd back at the ensign and snapped: "Admiral Dougherty is waiting for this. Transmit it to the ship."

Before he uttered the final word, the companel, set on audio, crackled loudly, and an excited Son'a voice shouted:

"Alert, area twelve!"

The blast of a weapon. Gallatin watched as the Ba'ku and their invisible observers turned toward the hills in astonishment.

On audio, the sound of scuffling; the thud of flesh striking flesh. A groan. The voice began speaking again, but the signal was breaking up. Gallatin could make out only a few garbled words.

". . . the android has . . ."

A burst of static. The realization of what could happen propelled Gallatin in a swift lunge to the nearest companel. He slammed a control with his fist. "Report!"

More static; gasping. The words: ". . . can't bring him down . . ."

Next to Gallatin, the pink-skinned ensign pointed,

following the gaze of the startled Ba'ku to the nearby foothills. "Over there!"

Invisible to the villagers, a figure in a glowing isolation suit was running down the rock-strewn hills with preternatural speed and agility.

Gallatin stepped toward the main viewscreen. "Magnify!"

The image bloomed abruptly, enlarging to reveal the foothills with such detail that Gallatin might have been there beside the fleeing figure as it scrambled down the steep hillside toward the village, preceded and followed by a small avalanche of stones and sand and dust. Two other glowing figures—Son'a, from their posture and movements—armed with plasma weapons gave chase. Alongside them ran a group of Ba'ku children, clearly terrified by the blast and entirely unaware that their path—also toward the village square—kept them in the midst of the invisible runners.

Something horrible had happened, Gallatin realized, with a heaviness in his heart, something that threatened the entire mission here. Even worse, that threatened to expose the deeper reasons for it to his Starfleet partners. Unlike the Federation scientists surrounding him, Gallatin knew that the first runner was Starfleet, and those following, Son'a. But there was still time; the Ba'ku had heard the blast, but probably only the children had actually seen it. If nothing else happened to arouse their suspicions, perhaps—

Too late. One of the Son'a guards lifted his plasma weapon and took aim at the fleeing figure. A streak of blinding brilliance surged toward the runner, barely missing him; at the accompanying thunder, the children shrieked.

On one of the companels that still showed the village square, the curly-haired Ba'ku woman demanded: "What is it? What's happening?" In her eyes and voice was more indignation than fright.

Anij, Gallatin remembered suddenly. *Your name is Anij, and of them all, you are the most fearless.* And he felt an intense, fleeting self-loathing.

Beside him, the Federation scientists rose as a group to their feet and watched with dismay as the chase continued down into the village; another eye-searing plasma blast caused the locals to scatter.

Gallatin's worst fears had come true; a Starfleet intruder had made an unfortunate discovery. By all rights, the Son'a should kill him. But if he permitted his people to kill a Starfleet officer here, in front of all these Starfleet scientists . . .

"Hold your fire!" he shouted at the com to the Son'a guards, then with a single look, conveyed an order to the Starfleet lieutenant seated beside him.

She knew immediately what he meant; she was quick-witted, intelligent, as were all the Starfleet personnel he had worked with; *and that,* he thought grimly, *is precisely the source of our problem now.*

She touched a control. "Base to Commander Data."

The voice that answered was halting, dazed—but not the least bit winded after the wild run. "Rerouting . . . microhydraulic . . . power distribution . . . regulating . . . thermal . . . overload . . ." On the viewscreen, the android ran staggering toward the village square.

Disoriented, damaged, Gallatin realized; perhaps there was a way out, after all. To destroy him gracefully, without insulting Starfleet.

"Data, report to base immediately," the lieutenant ordered.

If the android understood, he gave no sign; his mutterings seemed self-directed. "Transferring . . . positronic . . . matrix functions . . . engaging . . . secondary protocols . . ." As he ran, he lifted both gloved hands toward the neck of his helmet.

The Starfleet ensign who had handed Gallatin the padd cried out in horror: "He's trying to remove the headpiece!"

Gallatin tapped his own companel. "All field units. Intercept the android."

* * *

The boy Artim ran gasping through the village in search of his father . . . and an explanation. Father would explain it calmly; Father would lay his, Artim's, childish fears to rest. Sojef was old and wise and knew everything.

There *had* to be a simple explanation; there always was. Yet Artim could think of nothing at the moment that could account for the strange thunder he and his friends—Jusa, Nal, and the girls—had heard coming from down by the lake. Lightning, they all decided; but the sky was perfectly cloudless.

"Magic lightning," Nal suggested, and they had laughed at his foolish explanation. They were almost adults, after all; the changing time would soon be upon them, when the girls would no longer seem to be annoyances, but creatures of compelling interest. (Or so Father said, but to Artim the idea was still repellent.)

They had laughed, but then the girl Je'na had seen another impossibility: pebbles and dust, and clumps of grass trampled, as if someone invisible were *running* toward them.

"Look!" she had cried, pointing; *"look!"* And the fine hairs on Artim's neck and arms had lifted.

The disturbance passed, only to be followed by another—the same trampling of grass and stirring of dust, doubled—and all vestiges of Artim's maturity fled. He and the others broke into a run, away from the noise. *Ghosts,* he thought wildly; only ghosts could be so invisible; but ghosts were inhabitants of children's tales, not of reality.

Then the strange lightning split the air beside him, dazzling his eyes so that he closed them and saw streaks of blue. Lightning, yet not lightning; he could feel no electricity, smell no ozone. And with it came a boom of thunder so loud that his teeth rattled, and he shrieked like a shameless infant. All thoughts were banished save one.

Find Father . . .

Another blast; another roar of thunder.

Artim made it, sweating and gasping, past the pond and into the village, then the square. As he passed adults, he scanned their faces, hoping to find comfort—but saw instead only confusion.

And when at last he found Sojef directing others away from the approaching disturbance, Artim cried: "Father . . . ?"

It was a question, a demand for an answer, but there were no answers to be found in Sojef's expression. It was the same odd look that came upon him during those few times he had spoken of an earlier, evil time: when his own people had killed each other with weapons. What was the word for it? War.

And the look on Sojef's face had been fear.

Only Artim saw it there; only Artim knew his father

well enough. To the villagers, Sojef no doubt appeared the calm village leader.

But there was panic in the way he roughly grabbed Artim and held him tightly to him, as with his free arm, he directed his people toward the meeting hall: "Get inside! Find shelter!"

A loud splash behind them, as if someone had just plummeted into the pond.

Artim wriggled in his father's grasp and broke free, turning to look behind them just in time to witness the most impossible sight of all:

The floating head and neck of a man, barely more than an arm's length away. But not a man—at least, not Ba'ku. His skin was pale, shimmering gold, except for a deep, ugly wound across his neck—as if someone had branded him there with a white-hot poker.

His eyes were a bright, unnatural amber . . . and they stared directly at Artim.

The boy screamed and leaped backward, falling to the ground even as he struggled to turn and flee. Father had lied, lied to spare Artim the hideous truth that ghosts were *real,* and this particular one seemed to be after him . . . An angry ghost, perhaps murdered, decapitated by a hot poker.

Or worse, an offlander.

The other Ba'ku scattered at once; Father remained long enough to seize Artim's arm with painful strength and pull him away, just as the ghost's head spoke.

"Secondary protocols . . . active."

Not exactly what Artim had expected to hear. He let himself be dragged along, but could not help looking over his shoulder.

The head grimaced, grunted, as if fighting off invisible enemies. A noise Artim had never heard before, the ripping sound of a material somewhere between linen and metal, was followed by a flash of red, then the abrupt appearance of another man. At least, *part* of another man, head and torso in strange, torn clothing, suspended in the air beside the golden head. This second one seemed somewhat more Ba'ku, but he too was clearly offlander, his tight, masklike face mottled with ugly green sores.

In the middle of the square, these two wraiths battled hand-to-hand: the green-mottled man flailing out, his partially visible arms wrestling invisible ones beneath the golden ghost head.

Inside the duck blind, the Starfleet lieutenant half rose from her seat. "They can see him!"

"Stop him!" Gallatin bellowed, watching decades of work—and the very goal of his life—undone in seconds before his eyes. "Now!"

"Commander Data, stand down!" the lieutenant

shouted into the companel. "That's an order! I repeat: Stand down!"

Artim watched as the shrieking mottled man rose into the air, then plummeted down headfirst to the ground. There he lay, unconscious, while the golden head and scorched neck suddenly became a golden head, neck, torso, arms, and last of all, legs and feet. The first offlander parted the air as if it had been a cloak wrapped about him, and stepped forth from it.

In one swift, smooth move, he took the lightning weapon from the unconscious man's hands.

He will kill us now, Artim thought frantically; but instead, the golden man turned the weapon toward the bare rockface, and fired.

Something within the stone itself sputtered; the man fired again, again, again, each time filling the air with light and thunder.

The rockface shimmered as if made of moonbeams rather than mountain, then faded away to reveal a sight more impossible than any other Artim had yet seen.

In place of the rock was a small building sculpted from the stone, the front of which was entirely glass. And in the building were low black tables on which sat strange metal devices—squares that glowed different colors and displayed different pictures. Hiding

19

behind them were people, most of whom had apparently ducked for cover; as Artim and the rest of the astounded Ba'ku watched, those people rose slowly, sheepishly to their feet.

"What is it?" villagers murmured. "Who are they?"

Who, indeed? Artim wondered. Here was another mottled one, apparently a leader, dressed in garish purple-and-green robes, bejeweled with glittering gems and gold. Beside him stood a brown-skinned woman in a more sedate jumpsuit, just like the others, who were of different-colored skins and even of different species. They were clearly of one clan, and the mottled one of another.

A renewed wave of murmuring passed among the Ba'ku behind them, and Artim turned to see more offlanders there, dressed in the same bulky garb as the golden ghost had been.

As for the golden ghost, he lowered his weapon and stood surveying the results of his attack—not with maliciousness or hatred or any of the other emotions a homicidal ghost ought, Artim decided. If anything, the expression on his bland features was one of simple satisfaction.

TWO

☆

In the captain's quarters aboard the *U.S.S. Enterprise,*
Picard let go a sigh of disgust as his tenth attempt to
fasten the high, tight-fitting collar of his dress uniform
failed. Immediately, Beverly Crusher turned toward
him, caught both sides of the recalcitrant collar with
her thumbs, and gave it a yank that forced even more
air out of the captain's lungs. Picard shot her a dark
look, but she continued, undaunted, and with good
reason: they were running late.

Beside them, Troi—like the doctor and the captain,
attired in formal uniform—paused to glance up from
her padd, but wisely chose not to smile.

Wisely, Picard thought, because he himself was in
no mood to smile. The past several months had worn

him down, left him weary and irritable; he had not noticed it until Beverly had insisted he come in for an unscheduled medical exam.

I'm perfectly healthy, he'd insisted, and she'd replied:

You mean you're a perfect bear.

Cranky, that was the word she had used, a term that conjured up an image of himself as a sour-faced old geezer—emphasis on the *old*—and indeed, after the exam, she had admitted that Picard *was,* after all, perfectly healthy.

But not as young as you used to be. You're going to have to take some time off soon. Get some rest.

He'd been insulted. His irritation and tiredness had nothing to do with age; it had to do with all the myriad of diplomatic errands, the bureaucracy, the ridiculous flurry of low-priority assignments Starfleet had subjected them to of late. Captaincy of the *Enterprise* had become more like a high-stress business than an adventure. So many annoying details . . .

And he was not the only one to be tired lately; Beverly herself was looking rather wan. . . .

She had, of course, taken umbrage at that, which permitted him the wicked satisfaction of pointing out that perhaps *she* was the one who was cranky. But it was true; they were *all* tired and irritable. Weren't they?

Meanwhile, Troi continued the briefing. "The people are known as the Evora," she repeated, carefully articulating the pronunciation.

Beverly, too, seemed to be having great difficulty fastening the collar; if she pulled it any tighter, Picard decided, he would have to have an injection of tri-ox compound just to make it through the reception without asphyxiating.

". . . population three hundred million . . ." Troi droned on.

"Say the greeting again," Picard commanded. For some reason, his memory was no longer one hundred percent reliable of late.

"Yew-*cheen* chef-*faw*," Troi elaborated, glancing up at him. "Emphasis on the *cheen* and the *faw*."

Beverly suddenly clicked her tongue in disgust. "You need either a new uniform or a new neck."

He glanced beyond her at the bulkhead mirror and scowled. True, the skin of his neck was not as taut as it used to be, but he need only make a minor adjustment to his dietary and exercise programs to correct it. It had not changed; not as much as Beverly was suggesting. He was not *old* . . .

The door chimed; Troi discreetly avoided the topic of discussion by answering. Picard heard Will Riker's voice, but was not about to be distracted from correcting the doctor's unnecessarily snide remark.

"Yew-*cheen* chef-*faw*," he intoned, then snapped: "My collar size is exactly the same as it was at the Academy."

Beverly drew back to look at him with mock reassurance. *"Sure* it is." And in one brutal move that forced a gasp from him, she fastened the collar.

Dapper in formal dress with a freshly trimmed beard, Riker entered the room looking mildly sheepish. "Our guests have arrived and are eating the floral arrangements on the banquet tables."

Crusher arched an eyebrow. "I guess they don't believe in cocktails before dinner."

Picard drew a breath and, relieved that the collar did not pop open, strode out of the room and into the corridor at top speed.

The others followed. Dismayed, Troi scanned her padd for information. "Oh my God, are they vegetarians? That's not in here. . . ."

"Better have the chef whip up a light balsamic vinaigrette," Picard directed. "Something that goes well with chrysanthemums. Yew-*cheen* chef-*faw* . . .*"*

As he spoke, a feminine voice filtered through com. "Bridge to Captain Picard. . . ." He recognized it immediately—*so, my memory isn't going, after all*—as that of Kell Perim, a brilliant young Trill recently assigned to the *Enterprise.*

He answered without slowing his pace. "Yes, Ensign?"

24

"Command wants to know our ETA at the Goren system."

Picard frowned faintly at Riker. Command had been dumping missions on them fast and furious lately; this was just one more thing the captain hadn't had time to be briefed on yet. "The Goren system . . . ?"

Riker showed no outward sign of frustration, but Picard sensed it all the same, as his second-in-command replied, "They need us to mediate some territorial dispute."

"We *can't* delay the archeological expedition to Hanoran II," Picard countered, knowing that he was making his argument to the wrong person, and stating something Will knew all too well. "It would put us into the middle of monsoon season." He and the group rounded a pair of engineers working on a bulkhead panel.

Riker in turn responded with a fact his captain knew all too well: "The Diplomatic Corps is busy with Dominion negotiations."

It couldn't be helped, of course; but Picard sighed nonetheless. ". . . so they need us to put out one more brushfire." He paused to scan the faces of his entourage. "Anyone remember when we used to be explorers?"

No one answered; in silence, they all filed onto a turbolift. "Deck ten," Riker ordered.

Picard attempted to refocus himself, to summon up

whatever vestige of diplomatic charm remained in him. "Yew-*cheen* chef-*faw.*"

As if cued, Troi looked down at her padd to continue the briefing. "Remember, they have a significantly less advanced technology than ours. They only achieved warp drive last year."

"A year?" Crusher asked, mildly indignant. "And the Federation Council decided to make them a protectorate already?"

"In view of our losses to the Borg and the Dominion," Picard said, "the council feels we need all the allies we can get these days."

The turbolift doors parted abruptly, revealing the back entrance to the reception area filled with catering personnel, bearing fresh supplies of chrysanthemums and champagne, and ship's officers in dress uniform. From the reception suite itself came the sounds of violin music, laughter, and pleasant conversation.

Picard immediately realigned the muscles of his face into a more agreeable expression and stepped from the lift. Troi stayed at his side, still briefing.

"You'll be expected to dance with Regent Cuzar."

"Can she mambo?" Beverly asked, with a small, wicked smile.

"Very funny," Picard snapped, though his diplomatic smile never wavered. He studiously avoided Riker and Troi's bemused, questioning glances.

"Your captain used to cut quite a rug," Beverly began to explain, but she was blessedly interrupted by a female ensign who had noticed the group. "Captain on deck!"

The sea of officers also headed for the reception parted in front of them.

Another voice filtered through Picard's communicator. "La Forge to Picard. Captain, I need to talk to you before the reception—"

Picard drew a breath to reply . . .

And released it in surprise as he suddenly found himself face-to-face with Commander Worf.

"Captain," the Klingon acknowledged, in his resonant bass voice. He looked well, Picard decided; though it had been two years since they last had met in the desperate struggle against the Borg queen, Worf seemed not to have changed. His standard-issue uniform and Klingon sash (not to mention his fierce visage) distinguished him from the formal crowd. He still wore his hair long, pulled back at the nape of his neck; it seemed to Picard to have grown a few inches.

"Worf!" Picard exclaimed, at once confused and delighted. "What the hell are *you* doing here?" Last he'd heard, he still served on Deep Space 9.

The Klingon's stern expression lightened ever so slightly; it was the closest he could come to a smile. "I was at Manzar colony installing a new defense perimeter when I heard the *Enterprise* was in this sector."

As Worf spoke, Picard was equally aware of the com exchange between his second-in-command and chief engineer.

Riker: "He's a little late, Geordi. Can it wait?"

La Forge, firmly: "I don't think so, Commander."

Still in motion, Picard turned to Riker. "Tell him I'm already here . . . we can talk when he arrives."

Riker nodded, then addressed Geordi again: "The captain wants you to come over."

Without missing a beat, Picard returned his attention to Worf. There was no time for pleasantries now; they would have to come afterward. "I have a few ideas I'd like to discuss about Manzar security." Which was true enough, though Picard could have happily manufactured any of a dozen excuses to catch up with his former security officer. The Klingon nodded and excused himself. As the captain neared the banquet room, Riker remained a step behind, but Picard could still hear La Forge's voice on com:

"I'm on my way. Tell him we've received a communique from Admiral Dougherty."

Dougherty? Picard wondered. Dougherty was a seventy-ish, lower-level admiral from command who was overseeing the Ba'ku mission. *Please, not another assignment. How do they expect us to be three places at once?*

But he put the thought behind him. Now was the time to focus on the task at hand: he mentally checked his expression, straightened his tunic, and fought the urge to slip a finger between the damnably tight collar and his poor, pinched neck. With a gracious smile, he and his entourage stepped into the banquet room, where a string quartet launched into a spirited waltz. Between that, and the polite babble of voices Terran, Bajoran, Bolian, and Trill, he did not hear Geordi's final words:

"It's about Data."

As Picard entered the formal banquet area escorted by Counselor Troi, Crusher, and the now-in-step Riker, the crowd of Starfleet officers moved aside to give the captain's party access to the small Evora delegation.

Emphasis on the word *small.*

Picard's diplomatic smile faltered; through sheer will, he kept it from disappearing altogether. There had been nothing in Troi's briefing, nothing in the data provided by Starfleet, to suggest that the Evora were not within physical parameters suited to a humanoid-fitted ship.

The top of Cuzar's head, adornments included, barely came to the captain's waist. She was a matronly but elegant female, clad in sedate aubergine robes—in contrast to the more brightly dressed males who served her. Not one of them came as high as Picard's chest.

He knew Troi well enough to sense a very subtle change in her posture and expression; it had come as a surprise to her as well. Either someone at command had forgotten to relay the information, or deemed it unimportant.

Or worst, and most likely, they had realized that Picard would protest and argue on behalf of sending a different ship, one more appropriately sized so that the Evora would feel neither awkward nor uncomfortable with the accommodations. This is what came of command's recent hasty attitude.

Troi recovered smoothly, and with perfect graciousness bowed to the delegation. "Regent Cuzar, it is my honor to present to you the captain of the *Enterprise,* Jean-Luc Picard."

On cue, Picard added, "Yew-*cheen* chef-*faw,* Regent Cuzar. Welcome aboard the *Enterprise.*"

If Cuzar felt any discomfort due to her diminutive size, she hid it well; her mood seemed one of honest delight. With admirably regal bearing and an authoritative voice far deeper than Picard expected, she intoned, "Captain Picard, may I welcome you in the time-honored tradition of my people."

She signaled to a male aide, who stepped forward with an elaborate headdress adorned with crystalline beads, precious metals, and an unfortunate native bird's feathers. With consummate ceremony, she lifted it, and Picard realized with a thrill of dread that she would now crown him with it, apparently as a sign of respect . . . though he could not be sure. Troi had forgotten to mention this little detail—most likely because she knew the captain would complain about it.

It was the most awkward of ballets: Cuzar reaching as high as her arms would allow, Picard stooping as low as he could while maintaining the gesture's dignity, stretching the muscles in his hip in an effort to avoid a full squat. In the end, he barely avoided going into one—but only because Regent Cuzar was enough of a sport to rise on full tiptoe.

The headdress was, of course, too small; with valiant effort, she managed to perch it precariously atop his skull. Picard rose with extreme caution, lest he commit the unspeakable Evora faux pas of losing his crown. He felt like an idiot; the size difference was making a mockery of these people's tradition.

Yet to her credit, Cuzar appeared totally at ease and quite pleased with the result. With genuine warmth, she said, "We are so honored to be accepted within the great Federation family." A beat, then: "Please, I know you have other guests to greet."

Picard smiled at her and summoned whatever shred remained of his charm. "We have a dance later, I believe?"

"I look forward to it," Cuzar replied firmly. *An*

admirable liar and true diplomat, Picard decided, watching as one of her ministers led her away. And the instant she and the other Evora were out of earshot, he lifted gaze and eyebrows toward the wobbling headpiece and said sotto voce to Troi:

"Counselor?" His tone held a mild rebuke, a wry acknowledgment of her intentional omission.

Troi's expression remained studiously deadpan. "Nice beadwork."

"Excuse me, sir," Geordi La Forge interrupted, his tone one of concern. Picard glanced up to meet the gaze of his chief engineer's alabaster blue eyes—or rather, optical implants that reminded the captain of the blank white stare of Greek and Roman statues. Picard took the proffered padd and scanned it while La Forge explained. "Admiral Dougherty's aboard a Son'a ship in Sector four-four-one. He's requesting Data's schematics."

Picard looked up sharply at that, but it was Troi who voiced the concern. "Is something wrong?"

La Forge shook his head. "The message doesn't say."

There was something odd about the request, something subtly amiss that troubled the captain. The obvious explanation was that Data was suffering a serious malfunction, one the android could not correct by himself, and Dougherty was simply trying to help; and yet . . . Picard sensed something *wrong*. He lowered his voice. "Data should have been back by now. They were only scheduled to observe the Ba'ku village for a week." He looked pointedly at La Forge. "Set up a secured comlink to the admiral in the anteroom."

La Forge nodded shortly and moved off to comply. Picard had little time to worry; before he could take a single step, an enthusiastic and champagne-cheered Bolian officer seized his arm and began babbling.

"Captain, Hars Adislo, we met at the Nel Bato Conference last year; did you ever have a chance to read my paper on thermionic transconductance?"

Without the faintest glimmer of recognition, Picard smiled at him, then murmured hasty apologies. Dougherty's call might have caused him concern, but at least it provided rescue from polite conversation.

"He's not acknowledging any Starfleet protocols, not responding to any of our hails," Admiral Dougherty said. Picard had met him several times at various Starfleet functions, and taken orders from him twice: Matthew Dougherty, aged sixty-nine, silver-haired, lean, tanned; like all those in command, an excellent physical specimen and self-possessed charmer, looking years younger than his age. Conversation with him was always a delight—until last year, when his wife had passed away. She was retired Starfleet, Picard recalled, some three decades older than her husband, who had taken her death hard. He seemed recovered now, all business and confidence, but sorrow had definitely aged him, damped his exuberance; he appeared the near-septuagenarian that he was. The lines in his face appeared deeper, his eyes harder.

Picard absently fingered a feather on the Evora headpiece, which now sat on a console beside him. Next to him stood Geordi La Forge; outside the open doorway, an ensign stood in order to steer curious banquet-goers away.

"You have no idea what precipitated his behavior?" Picard asked of Dougherty; they spoke of Data, who according to Son'a witnesses had gone berserk and starting firing at shielded cultural observers. The worst that could possibly go wrong on a no-contact cultural mission had—the natives, in this case the Ba'ku, had witnessed the shoot-out and decloaking of observers, thus becoming aware of the technologically advanced Federation in the most alarming way possible.

Dougherty shook his head. "And now he's holding our people hostage down there . . ."

The captain paused. The chances of positronic circuitry spontaneously corrupting were infinitesimal at best; if what Dougherty was saying were true, that

Data had turned into a rogue android on the rampage—and Picard had no reason to believe it was not—then surely Data had suffered some sort of physical trauma. The admiral insisted the android had not—but then, Dougherty knew only as much as certain witnesses had told him.

But Picard sensed where the argument was heading. If Data presented a grave danger to the other personnel, and no one there could figure out how to deal with his circuitry, it would be far too easy to justify his destruction. Crusher and Geordi, with their years of experience in dealing with the android, needed to be there.

"The *Enterprise* can be at your position in two days, Admiral."

"That's not a good idea," Dougherty countered swiftly. "Your ship hasn't been fitted for this region; there are environmental concerns—"

Picard frowned. "What kind of concerns?"

Dougherty broke off eye contact briefly to study a point some two feet above Picard's left shoulder. "We haven't fully identified the anomalies yet." He once again met Picard's gaze. "They're calling this whole area the Briar Patch. Took us a day to reach a location where we could get a signal out to you. Just get me Data's schematics. I'll keep you informed. Dougherty out."

Picard acknowledged with a nod; the viewscreen image faded to that of a Federation logo. He turned from it to La Forge. "His emotion chip?"

The engineer shook his head. "Didn't take it with him."

Picard paused. "Send the admiral Data's schematics."

In the periphery of his vision, La Forge nodded assent. There was no time to head for the Briar Patch, of course—any more than there was time to get the archeological expedition to Hanoran II before the monsoons began while taking care of the situation brewing in the Goren system. But it was time to prioritize—and Picard knew with indescribable, illogical certainty that whatever was happening in the Briar Patch with the Ba'ku mission—and to Data—took precedence over all. Something was wrong; Dougherty had been too quick, too adamant, in his insistence that the *Enterprise* not be involved.

Picard looked over his shoulder and called softly, "Ensign . . ."

"Sir?" The young Bajoran male entered at once.

"Report to the galley and tell the chef to skip the fish course."

The ensign looked mildly askance at this, then turned without further question and exited. Picard turned back toward the monitor to see Geordi's pale implants regarding him curiously.

"I want our guests to depart as quickly as etiquette allows," the captain explained. "I'll ask Worf to delay his return to Deep Space 9 so he can join us. We're going to stop by Sector four-four-one on our way to the Goren system."

La Forge caught on immediately. "They . . . *are* in opposite directions, sir."

"Are they?" Picard asked dryly.

La Forge flashed a small but brilliant smile at him before leaving. Alone, Picard stared at the Evora headdress beside him. As worried as he was about Data, the incident had at least provided an excuse to avoid more of the busywork command kept handing him. It had weighed him down of late; he felt worn, irritable . . . old. Life was too short to waste doing meaningless things.

With a sigh, he picked up the headdress and set it upon his head, and in an act of sheer will forced a smile.

THREE

In the body-enhancement facility aboard the Son'a ship, Matthew Dougherty struggled to hide his disgust at Starfleet's new allies. The room itself made him uncomfortable enough; it smacked of an old nineteenth-century Earth bordello, with its scarlet velvet veils, ornate gold-pressed latinum fixtures, and low lighting. A brothel-cum-sickbay, with reclining Son'a figures receiving transfusions of reportedly rejuvenating chemicals. It even had scantily clad women, clearly there as slaves and sex objects, and that alone was enough to trouble him. He sat straight, prim in his understated admiral's uniform, upon a couch made for reclining, and reminded himself that, while he personally did not agree with the Son'a that abject hedonism was a virtue, he was still bound to treat them civilly.

Beside him, Ru'afo, the Son'a commander titled the ahdar, lay back languidly and enjoyed the skilled attentions of a pair of female aestheticians: one of the Tarlac race, the other of the Ellora, both dressed in skimpy tunics designed for distraction, not function. And Ru'afo was letting himself be shamelessly distracted—and looking quite amused by Dougherty's obvious discomfort. Like his peers, the ahdar was draped in shimmering fabrics and myriads of latinum chains bearing the largest collection of precious jewels Dougherty had ever seen outside a museum; the ubiquitous mirrors before which the race constantly preened doubled the glittering effect. Of all the Son'a, Ru'afo disgusted him most of all; had Ru'afo had his way, the Son'a would simply have gone in with their plasma weapons and rounded up the Ba'ku without the slightest consideration of the respect due sentient beings.

But at the moment, it was Ru'afo who was annoyed with the admiral. The Son'a spoke heatedly while his two alien attendants massaged oils and creams into his cheeks and forehead. The sweet, intoxicating floral aroma wafting up from him contrasted with the harshness of his tone.

"I should never have let you talk me into the duck blind in the first place," the ahdar proclaimed. His indignation thoroughly incensed Dougherty, who, at the same time that he worked to master his temper, also found himself unwillingly fascinated by Ru'afo's skin—or at least, that part of it not covered with cream or delicate fingertips. So overstretched and thin it was that each individual capillary, brightly abloom now with anger, could be clearly traced. "Your Federation procedures have made this mission ten times as difficult as it needed to be!"

"Our procedures were in place to protect the planet's population from unnecessary risk," Dougherty countered, priding himself on his even tone.

"Planet's population," the Son'a scoffed, in a tone that Dougherty, accustomed to the respect due an admiral, had not heard in years. "Six hundred people. You want to avoid unnecessary risks? Next time leave your android home."

At the dressing-down, Dougherty felt a sudden heat upon his cheeks and neck. He literally bit his tongue to avoid answering sharply; Ru'afo's group was even smaller than the Ba'ku's, insignificant and unremarkable, save for their reputation as petty criminals. Starfleet was dealing with them only because they now possessed a technology the Federation lacked. *The minute we have what we need from them . . .* Dougherty promised himself silently. Until then, he would remain civil to this arrogant alien.

Fortunately, a voice filtered through Ru'afo's personal comlink, sparing Dougherty the necessity of a reply.

"Bridge to Ahdar Ru'afo. We're approaching the planet."

With a disinterested, jaded air, Ru'afo signaled for the cosmeticians to finish, then pressed his comlink. "Take us into high orbit." He rose, then turned to Dougherty, shifting from anger to hospitality as he proffered his now-vacant chair. "Lie down, Admiral. The girls will take twenty years off your face."

Twenty years. Ru'afo appeared a few years younger than the admiral, if that, and he spent at least an hour with the aestheticians every day.

"Another time," Dougherty replied stonily, and rose.

The Son'a shrugged as he paused to study the facial's effects on his complexion in the nearest mirror. Glancing at Dougherty's reflection, he murmured, "Your self-restraint puzzles me, Admiral. You continue to deny yourself every benefit this mission has to offer."

"I prefer to wait until we can share the benefits with all the people of the—"

Federation was the last word Dougherty said, but neither he nor the others heard it. The deck beneath his feet suddenly shuddered, accompanied by a loud *boom*. Dougherty had served his years as a captain, and known combat; he had not forgotten the sound and feel of a phaser blast.

Ru'afo apparently knew it too; he glanced knowingly at Dougherty, and was out the door and on the lift without a word. Dougherty kept pace with him every step of the way. He knew the origin of the blast, of course, for he had surmised the details Ru'afo had omitted from the account, and he had familiarized himself with every Starfleet officer assigned the Ba'ku mission. But he maintained silence until the time was right.

The Son'a bridge—or rather, the sumptuous parlor that served as a bridge, with its latinum-plated consoles and the ahdar's fur-lined chair—irritated Dougherty the instant he and Ru'afo stepped from the turbolift; the flashing purple alert lights hurt his eyes. On the main screen, the ringed planet of the Ba'ku rotated lazily, half-obscured by phenomena common to the Briar Patch: rose-colored plasma tendrils, adrift in the ocean of space like Terran jellyfish, and translucent mother-of-pearl gas clouds.

"Report," Ru'afo ordered as he took his chair; the admiral stood beside him.

The entire bridge crew were either Tarlac or Elloran, save for two Son'a officers, one male and one female. The male Son'a, apparently Ru'afo's Number One, replied quickly. "Phaser blast. Unknown origin."

"Raise shields," Ru'afo ordered. As Elloran officers at the console hastened to comply, another blast shook the ship. Dougherty took a few wildly swaggering steps before he managed to catch hold of a console and balance.

Ru'afo's tone rose. "Take us out of orbit." He was concerned, Dougherty knew, about taking another hit. While the vessel's shields could probably afford another phaser blast—the dying race's technology was second to none—every Son'a Dougherty had ever met avoided even minor physical injury to an extreme degree. Indeed, the language had no word for "death." It was referred to by euphemism only, and then in whispers, briefly, as if it were the most heinous crime.

Before the death of his wife, Madalyn, Dougherty, in his naive arrogance, would have thought them unnaturally phobic; now he understood. And would do almost anything to help others avoid the same cruel pain.

"Photon torpedoes!" a Tarlac officer shouted. "Brace for impact!"

Dougherty rested his chest upon the console and held on, one arm grasping the edge in front of him, the other arm holding on to the side. Before the ship could move out of range, the first blow hit.

This strike was hardest. The ship reeled; Dougherty's ears popped, then shrieked, at the noise—too loud, too overwhelming to specify as any particular type of sound, to describe as anything other than pain. Through miraculous effort, Dougherty kept his grip on the console.

And then the hits came again, again, again. Dougherty held on, slipping only once to his knees; a quick glance at Ru'afo showed the Son'a in the grip of both terror and fury as he clutched the arms of his command chair. The admiral heard the sizzle of sparks at consoles behind him, smelled acrid smoke, saw in the periphery of his vision bodies tumbling to the deck. The lights flickered, leaving the bridge briefly in darkness.

It occurred to Dougherty that he might actually die here, now. He was not naive enough to believe that he would join Madalyn in some distant, nebulous paradise; nevertheless, dying now did not seem a bad thing. He was tired of loneliness, of grief.

Abruptly, the blows ceased.

"The vessel has broken off pursuit, sir," one of the Son'a officers reported behind him.

"Visual contact!" a female Elloran called, her face ghostly behind wisps of smoke.

Ghostly, too, was the sight of the attacking ship on the main screen, half hidden by a semitransparent gas cloud. As it sailed free of the cloud, Dougherty gasped. "That's *our* ship."

The small Federation scoutship turned and sailed

back toward the Ba'ku planet surface; although its pilot could not be seen from the Son'a vessel, Dougherty had no doubt as to his identity:

The android, Commander Data.

At that very instant in the *Enterprise* captain's quarters, surrounded by the strains of Beethoven's *Sonata Pathétique* as well as padds and star charts, Picard sat thinking about Admiral Dougherty.

"Tea," he demanded of the replicator beside him, without taking his gaze from the padd on his desk. "Earl Grey. Hot." He was still reading when the fragrance of bergamot prompted him to reach out blindly and take cup and saucer.

What possible reason could Matthew Dougherty have for wanting to keep the *Enterprise* away? His excuse of "environmental concerns" didn't hold water; if the area of space surrounding the Ba'ku planet was *that* dangerous, why had Picard heard nothing of it? Data had not mentioned it himself, when he was assigned to the mission, and a large contingent of Starfleet personnel had been there for a matter of weeks—as had Dougherty himself. If it was safe enough for Fleet officers for an extended stay, surely it was safe enough for the *Enterprise* crew to spend *one* day offering the specialized knowledge of Data only they possessed.

No, it had to be something else. Picard had even

checked with command; the Ba'ku project was entirely unclassified. Even if it weren't, Picard's security clearance was as high as the admiral's. They had no reason to hide anything from him.

What, then? Dougherty's record was beyond reproach; surely he would never involve himself in anything of questionable legality. Could he be in some danger from the Son'a? Picard knew little of the race; what little he had heard was not complimentary.

At the very least, Data was in definite trouble—and so were those he might attack. If the android was truly on the rampage, it was only a matter of time before he seriously injured or—God forbid—killed someone. And when that happened, Dougherty and the Son'a would be within their rights to terminate him.

Picard wanted desperately to get there before such a thing occurred—but from the looks of the Briar Patch, it would be impossible for the *Enterprise* to make it to the Ba'ku planet quickly. Space travel in the Patch was the equivalent of wading through waist-high mud.

He frowned at the padd, whose readout listed all anomalies present in the Patch, then rose, tea in one hand, padd in the other, and walked over to his dining table. It, too, was littered with stacks of padds, charts, and maps. Still focused on the readout, he sat down in front of a half-eaten salad and propped the padd on the other research materials to better see it. Thus situated, he ate a forkful of salad, then took a sip of tea, peripherally aware that it was good to be working on a genuine problem again.

There had to be some way to make it through more quickly—some shortcut, some wormhole, *something* that would allow the *Enterprise* to arrive on the scene before harm came to Data or anyone else. Surely he had missed something. . . . Picard half-rose and reached for a readout on the planet—

—upsetting the salad plate. Pieces of lettuce, arugula, watercress, scattered onto table, floor, padds, Picard himself; dressing spilled onto his jacket, dousing him with the pungent aroma of aged cheese. Concentration broken at last, he sighed and brushed an oily piece of lettuce from his lap.

At that instant, the door chimed. Of course.

"Who is it?" Picard demanded.

"Commander Riker."

Picard looked down at himself, assessing the damage, and shrugged. "Come. Computer, end music."

The first movement of the sonata ceased abruptly as Riker entered with a padd. Will's gaze was immediately drawn to the captain's stained tunic; the first officer's expression remained sober enough, but Picard knew him well enough to sense the playful grin that lurked just beneath the surface.

"I'm a casualty of a working lunch," he explained unnecessarily. He rose and took off his tunic while Riker watched in slightly *too* respectful silence. As Picard moved to his cabinet, disposed of the dirtied tunic, and pulled on a clean one, he continued talking. "I've been going over the few star charts we have of this Briar Patch. It's full of supernova remnants, false vacuum fluctuations . . ."

". . . and Gorgonzola cheese," Riker added smoothly, bending down to flick a piece of errant cheese from a chart.

Picard ignored him. "We won't be able to go any faster than one-third impulse in that muck."

Riker straightened as the amusement in his eyes faded. All business, he handed Picard a padd. "Nothing dangerous turned up in the astrometric survey."

Picard glanced stunned at the readout, a new question now taking precedence in his mind. Why had Matthew Dougherty lied to him? "So where are the environmental concerns the admiral was talking about?"

Riker shrugged, as if trying to deflect the captain's unspoken question, but his gaze acknowledged the serious implications his statement raised. "The only unusual readings were low levels of metaphasic radiation from interstellar dust across the region."

Radiation that was harmless even at full exposure. Picard returned Riker's look, but said nothing; there was nothing to say, not until they arrived on the Ba'ku planet and made their own investigation.

It was Worf, on com, who broke the silence. "Bridge to Captain Picard. We are approaching Sector four-four-one."

"Slow to impulse," Picard ordered. "We're on our way."

On the bridge viewscreen, the Briar Patch glowed with the incandescent magnificence of a thousand Terran sunsets: glittering serpentine coils of plasma snaked languidly through pearlescent clouds of gas, dust, and rubble, the legacy of long-dead stars. At the same time that Picard appreciated its beauty, he cursed its treachery: once within its grasp, the *Enterprise* would be hobbled, cut off from all outside contact.

As Picard stepped off the lift with Riker at his side, he noted with a sense of nostalgia the presence of Worf at tactical. Troi and La Forge were waiting at their respective stations of command and ops. The new Trill ensign, Kell Perim, sat at conn.

La Forge turned from his post. "We're about to lose communications with Starfleet, Captain."

Picard acknowledged with a look, then, accompanied by Riker, moved over to the command station and addressed the seated Counselor Troi. "Do you have everything you need from command?"

She nodded. "We've downloaded all the files on the duck blind mission and the Son'a."

He drew Riker into the conversation with a glance and said to them both: "You have two days to become experts." The counselor and second-in-command were best suited to remain aboard the ship and deal with the no-doubt disgruntled Son'a. "Mister Worf . . . our job will be to find a plan to safely capture Data."

In response, the Klingon held up a tricorder that had positronic circuitry attached. "I've already had Commander La Forge modify a tricorder with one of Data's actuation servos. Its operational range is only four meters, but it will shut him down."

Picard smiled in honest appreciation of the Klingon's initiative. "It's good to have you back, Worf." He sat, and told Perim: "Slow to one-third. Take us in."

It was in the *Enterprise* library, amid the monitors and force-shielded, climate-controlled shelves of ancient paper tomes, that Will Riker began to feel the first effects. He and Deanna Troi were sitting at parallel stations in an area where several other silent researchers were working. Deanna picked the Son'a's recent interest in the Ba'ku planet, and their joint mission with Starfleet; Will volunteered to cover culture and history.

At the moment, Deanna was briefing him on her discoveries; and for the first time in years, Riker was suddenly intoxicated by the scent of gardenias—in fact, he felt as giddy as if he'd been drinking real, not synthetic, alcohol. It was a scent she had worn long ago, when they were first lovers. She wore it in her hair, and he was not sure whether she washed with it or wore it as perfume. Either way, he felt an overwhelming urge to touch her soft, dark hair, to lift it to his face . . .

He straightened in his chair and forced himself to concentrate on what she was saying. What *was* she saying? Something about the Son'a discovering the Ba'ku planet six months ago . . .

"Turned out it's in Federation space," Deanna continued in a low voice, "so they came to us to get approval for a sociological study. The Federation Council suggested it be a joint mission."

Riker managed to shake off the effect of the perfume enough to ask, "Why was Data assigned?"

"Environmental concerns, again." She turned back toward her monitor, displaying the profile of a classic dark-eyed beauty, and briefly forgot to lower her tone. "An android could be safely exposed to the elements during the installation of a duck blind—"

"*Sssshhh . . .*"

The harsh whisper made them both turn to see one of the librarians—this one a middle-aged human female who struck Riker as being prune-faced. He fought back a grin; here they were, Number One and the ship's counselor, getting shushed like a couple of high-school kids.

Troi ducked her head guiltily and went back to her reading, this time playing distractedly with the notepad of paper kept beside each monitor for emergency scribbling.

Riker huddled closer to her—*the better to smell you, my dear*—and whispered softly, "I don't see anything to suggest the Son'a have any interest in sociology."

She turned toward him, curious. "What *are* they interested in?"

He grinned at his monitor. "Wine, women, and song."

Deanna sniffed primly. "You should feel right at home with them."

Something small and nearly weightless struck his temple on the side where she sat; he looked down and saw a little paper ball, rolled from the scratchpad. Riker turned, amused and indignant, to face his attacker, and saw her looking innocently at her computer screen.

Too innocently. *This means war.*

"Nomadic," he whispered, reading from his own screen, while he busily rolled his own paper ball. "Collectors of precious metals, jewels . . ."

"Hmmm," Deanna purred teasingly. *"I* should feel right at home with them . . ."

"You're in luck," Riker said, feeling the giddiness sweep over him again; he really *did* feel like a kid in a high-school library. "They use alien women as indentured servants." At her scathing look, he added innocently: "A half-century ago, they conquered two primitive races, the Tarlac and the Ellora, and then integrated them into their culture as a labor class." He gave his hidden-from-view paper ball a final good roll, and lifted his forearm to loft it—

—and just then noticed the prune-faced librarian looking daggers at him.

Caught. He turned sheepishly back to his computer screen and began reading again. What he found made him recoil slightly in surprise; he turned to Deanna, and inclined his head at his monitor. "Look at *this.*"

She rose from her seat and leaned over Riker's shoulder, supporting herself with one arm on the console.

"The Son'a are known to have produced mass quantities of the narcotic ketracel-white," Riker read in a whisper, "their ships are rumored to be equipped with isolytic subspace weapons *outlawed* by the Second Khitomer Accord . . ."

"Why would we be involved with these people?" Deanna asked, and Will was suddenly keenly aware of something soft and warm leaning against his upper arm: her breast.

"Good question," he replied blankly, and swallowed with a faintly audible *gulp*. All intelligible thought fled him as he told himself, panicked by the heat of his reaction: *Don't assume she's flirting with you and say something stupid; she's just innocently leaning against you and doesn't realize—*

One glance up at her convinced him otherwise; they exchanged a look that was pure heat. Riker broke off eye contact almost instantly and fixed his attention back on the screen. Okay, so at the moment he had entirely forgotten the reason for their breakup and knew himself to be an utter fool for ever having let this amazing, beautiful woman go.

Back to the Son'a. He continued to scan the information scrolling past on his screen, but could not ignore—did not *want* to ignore—the delicious, gooseflesh-inducing way she began to play with the hair at the nape of his neck.

"You haven't done that in a long time," he breathed.

She leaned against him, closer; the dark perfumed hair swung down and brushed his ear, and he drew in the scent of flowers as she murmured, "What . . . ?"

"What you're doing to my neck . . ."

Her tone was playful; he heard rather than saw the little smirk she wore. "Was I doing something to your neck?"

Something on the screen caught his eye, distracted him; he paused the scrolling. "It says here that some form of genetic anomaly has prevented the Son'a from procreating."

"No *children?*"

Riker nodded. "If that's true, they're a dying race." He paused, reading further—then winced at the sudden sharp *ping* against his cheek. A paper ball, rolled tight and hard; he looked up and saw sitting nearby a Trill ensign with a torn notepad looking—too innocently—at his monitor.

"Hey," Riker said loudly—and instantly realized he had caught the attention of everyone in that section of the library, including Old Pruneface herself. She had risen from her chair and was glaring at both Riker and Troi.

And Deanna, the little snitch, pointed at him accusingly. *"He* started it."

Riker raised his hands in protest. "I didn't do anything, I swear it."

But the glaring Medusa clearly did not believe; in the face of her implacable glare, Riker surrendered and left. He and Deanna had finished their mission there, and he was in a panic to head for the safety of the bridge—before he forgot he was on duty and swept her off to his quarters.

FOUR

☆

In the secure darkness of his *Enterprise* guest quarters, Worf dreamed he wrestled a young male Kolar beast.

The creature's size matched Worf's, though its body was thick and pudgy, all bones and sharp angles hidden by a layer of what appeared to be fat. Toothless, it was covered by a short layer of silvery, down-soft fur, and given its head—flat-skulled, long-snouted, be-whiskered—and its wide, softly startled eyes, Worf deemed it most similar in appearance to the Terran gray seals he had once seen sunning along the mountainous coastline of northern California.

Unlike the seals, however, the Kolar beast stood erect on powerful haunches, and its black gums were capable of crushing Klingon bone to powder; each of its stubby arms terminated in a row of a dozen claws. Claws needle-thin, but strong and sharp enough to shred flesh in a single swipe.

Kolar beasts were favored by adolescent Klingons seeking to prove their courage and strength—for the creature's thick padding was not fat, but pure, sinewy muscle. Its favorite methods of killing foolish young Klingons was by either suffocation (the muscles in its midsection were prehensile, capable of engulfing either side of its prey and slowly squeezing it to death) or disembowelment with its surgically keen claws.

At the moment, those claws whizzed by Worf's ears, slicing the air with a high-pitched, deadly sound, even as the Klingon pinned back the beast's arms; the slavering black gums thudded together with deafening, head-reeling thunder. Worf had wedged the top of his skull beneath the animal's jawbone—a near-perfect fit, the best manner in which to subdue a Kolar—and now bored into it with all his might, forcing the neckless beast's chin (and deadly jaws) up, away. Face pressed against the pungent, animal flesh of its short neck, Worf himself snapped—biting into striated muscle as hard as stone. There was a soft spot hidden here, if only he could find it in time. But even as he bit, the Kolar's belly muscles were undulating, expanding, slowly engulfing the sides of Worf's ribs, beginning to apply pressure, until they began audibly to crack . . .

At the same time, the beast's claws *snicked* forward, tearing into Worf's right deltoid and pulling away large shreds of violet, bloody flesh. At the hot smell of his own blood, Worf snarled in pain—

—fiery, exhilarating, glorious pain—

—and in a daring move, kicked out with both feet, finding the tender spot at the juncture of abdomen and haunch. The beast roared, lost its balance, fell hard onto its back, belly muscles suddenly slack. This was the instant when most challengers met death, losing their hold on the animal's arms or neck—but with a warrior's grace, Worf held on perfectly, his bite on the Kolar's neck never loosening.

Once down, the creature's low center of gravity did not permit it to rise; furious, keening, it champed its jaws harder, harder, until hot, acrid foam streamed onto Worf's head, down his face, stinging his eyes. The Klingon lay spread-eagled atop its muscular bulk, his knees digging into the tender spots that disabled its legs, his hands clutching its arms, his teeth pulling, ripping through the rock-hard muscle of its neck, searching for the one delicate area . . .

At last, he found it: an eye-sized soft spot of downy

flesh. He bit into it, and blood—hot, bitter, salty— spurted against the roof of his mouth, onto his tongue, down his throat. He howled, intoxicated, and drank.

And when he had had his fill, his mouth and face dripping with the Kolar's wine-colored blood, he crawled off the beast and was suddenly overwhelmed with desire.

He looked up at the sound of laughter—not mocking or amused, but victorious—and saw before him the long-dead K'Ehleyr, the mother of his son, now resurrected. How young she seemed, how strong and fiercely beautiful, how Klingon. She stood, arms akimbo, grinning slyly—and at the realization that she was seen, she laughed again and tossed her hair, as if daring him.

So. I die, and all you can do is take up with measly pale-skinned excuses for females: Betazoid, Trill. Do you remember what it is to love a real woman, a Klingon? Touch me gently, kiss me tenderly, and I'll tear your arms from their sockets.

He reached for her—

Bridge to Commander Worf.

K'Ehleyr's image paled, wavered; growling, he tried to seize it and touched something cold, hard, metallic . . . a ship's bulkhead. At the same time, he became vaguely conscious of a distant bleating that had continued for some time. The shriek of a *djabi* bird, he had assumed—but no, this sound was mechanically persistent.

His sleep alarm. It was trilling—and had been for some time. He had overslept.

The realization pierced the veil of his unconsciousness. He opened his eyes to darkness and sat, panicked—had he dreamed it, or had Picard actually called him from the bridge?

"Worf?" The captain's tone conveyed annoyance.

"Captain . . ." he gasped, mortified. In all his years with Starfleet, he had never—

"I don't know how they do it on Deep Space 9," Picard stated dryly, "but on the *Enterprise,* we still report for duty on time."

In reply, Worf rose swiftly in the darkness—promptly bumping his crown on the low ceiling over his bunk. He had forgotten about that particular quirk in the *Enterprise*'s officer cabins and that—plus his unthinkable sin of oversleeping—troubled him. As did the inebriating surge of adrenaline and passion at the memory of the Kolar's blood in his mouth, at the memory of K'Ehleyr with arms open wide, waiting for him.

He felt like a youth, he realized, as he hurriedly pulled on uniform, boots, sash (he had slept in his uniform); a youth lusting for battle, and love . . . And he remembered with sudden clarity how, when he was in the throes of adolescence, sleep had come so heavily upon him that none could wake him.

It took Worf mere seconds to dress; as he strode out the door into the corridor, he realized the comlink had not been severed; the captain was still awaiting an answer.

"I . . . I must have slept through my alarm," the Klingon said to com. "I'm on my way. . . ."

Even as he spoke, the sensations of passion and ferocity evoked by the dream followed him, and he wondered: What was in the air aboard the *Enterprise,* that he should feel so?

On the bridge, meanwhile, Picard had already arrived at his own explanation: It was the mission to save Data, and the clear sense of purpose, that filled him with exceptional energy that morning.

"We'll skip the court-martial this time," he told the dazed Worf. "Picard out." And he looked up at the bridge—at La Forge at ops, Kell Perim at conn, Lieutenant Daniels at tactical—and was pleased.

The captain had risen early and exercised—fencing, today—with especial fervor, pleased to find all lassitude, all sense of boredom and weariness, dissolved. He felt (dare he think it?) *young.* All of Beverly's pointed comments about his aging, and indeed, his own observations that confirmed she was right, were entirely wrong. Aging had nothing to do with his increasing physical and mental tiredness—all of it, even the deepening creases in his forehead, was gone after one night's rest. Perhaps it was his imagination, but even his sight and hearing seemed slightly improved.

To test the latter, he relaxed himself and focused on the faint hum of the engines. He had grown so used to them over the years that most times he was unaware of them, just as he was unaware of the sound of his own breath—but he knew both well enough to detect any irregularity.

And there one was—a barely audible, high-pitched whine buried within the deeper, constant hum. He lifted an eyebrow, rose, and stepped forward to La Forge's and Perim's stations. "When was the last time we aligned our torque sensors?"

Perim glanced over her shoulder at him. "Two months ago, sir."

The captain frowned. "They don't sound right."

Both reacted swiftly to the pronouncement, fingers flying over consoles as they each ran diagnostics; both reached the same conclusion at the same time, and stared up at each other in mild surprise.

La Forge at last looked over at his captain. "The torque sensors *are* out of alignment—by twelve *microns*. You could *hear* that?"

Picard permitted himself a self-satisfied little smile.

"When I was an ensign, I could detect a *three*-micron misalignment. . . ."

"Excuse me, Sir," Lieutenant Daniels interrupted. "The Son'a ship with Admiral Dougherty aboard has entered tracking range."

Amazing, Picard thought, with a glance at the Briar Patch's murky, beautiful clouds and debris onscreen, that the sensors could detect anything at all in this pea soup. "Try to hail them."

Daniels complied as the bridge doors opened and a sheepish Worf entered, his sash twisted, half-backward. "Admiral Dougherty responding," Daniels said, rising as the Klingon moved to replace him. Worf settled into the station as Daniels exited the bridge.

Picard gave Worf a pointed sidewise glance. "Straighten your baldric, Commander," he said sternly, with no small amount of hidden amusement. "On screen . . ."

He had been prepared, of course, by Riker and Troi's briefing on the Son'a's appearance and culture—as well as their less-than-ethical involvement with the drug and slave trade. Or Picard had thought; but he still found distaste welling up in him at the sight of the Son'a sitting next to Dougherty. This would be Ru'afo, the Son'a commander or ahdar.

He was older, around Dougherty's age—or perhaps older than the admiral, for whatever youth the

Son'a still possessed was definitely born of artifice. The skin of his face was pulled taut over the bone structure (only part of which he had probably been born with), giving him the appearance of a slightly startled skeleton; a large scar, where the skin had apparently torn many times, marred his forehead. Ru'afo's eyes were old, mistrustful, calculating—and as full of glittering artifice as his jewel-encrusted tunic, designed to push any less-than-youthful girth into more pleasing lines.

As for Matthew Dougherty, he appeared ill at ease in the sumptuously appointed setting; and even more ill at ease to be looking at Picard. His manner was far from cordial. "Captain, I wasn't expecting you."

"This was too important for the *Enterprise* to be on the sidelines, Admiral," Picard countered. Dougherty had never given him a direct order forbidding him to come; he had merely discouraged him. What had he said exactly?

That's not a good idea. . . . Just get me Data's schematics.

Picard had responded promptly to the one order; he'd provided the admiral with schematics immediately. Technically, Dougherty could not accuse him of insubordination, and they both knew it.

Displeased the admiral might be; but Picard knew him to be a reasonable, compassionate man, who surely understood the captain's concern for a crew member. Dougherty sighed deeply, and his expression shifted from one of discomfort to one of sympathy.

Ru'afo's remained calculating, glittering.

"I wish I had better news," Dougherty said. "Commander Data attacked us in the mission scoutship yesterday. Ru'afo and I have decided to send in an assault team."

"Sir," Picard answered swiftly, "Commander Worf and I have been working on several tactical plans to safely—"

"Your android has turned dangerously violent, Captain," the Son'a said, lunging forward in his latinum-plated chair with the fury of a coiled serpent on the verge of striking. "Considerable damage was done to my ship. He must be destroyed."

Dougherty's tone remained kindly but implacable. "I know what Data means to Starfleet, Jean-Luc, but our crew is at the mercy of those people on the planet. Because of Data's wild attacks, they think we mean to harm them, and they're holding our entire mission team down there. The effects on the Ba'ku are bound to be unfathomable, but if they harm any of the hostages—well, you can see how delicate the situation is. We can't afford for anyone else to interfere. And if, God forbid, Data kills one of the Ba'ku—"

Picard replied in a voice soft, low, steely. "If our

first attempt to capture Data fails, I will terminate him." He paused. "I should be the one to do it. I'm his captain . . . and his friend."

Dougherty clearly heard and understood; Ahdar Ru'afo's expression was one of pure hostility. "It isn't safe for you to remain in this area," the Son'a said.

Dougherty gave his unlikely cohort a sidewise glance, then told Picard, "He's right. Our shields have been upgraded to protect against the environmental anomalies. . . ."

Picard held firm. "We haven't noticed any ill effects."

Dougherty studied him a long beat. It was clear that he and Ru'afo were far from friends, and had probably been at odds since the first day the Ba'ku mission began; Picard did not envy Dougherty the assignment. But it was also clear that, for some unspoken reason, the Son'a did not want the *Enterprise* here—a reason to which the admiral was also sympathetic.

Picard watched as Dougherty wavered, then made his decision. "All right," the admiral said. "You have twelve hours, Captain, to retrieve your android, and no more. Then I want you *out* of the Briar Patch. In the meantime, we'll be heading out to the perimeter to call for Son'a reinforcements in case you fail. Remember—retrieve Data, then get out."

"Understood," Picard answered gratefully.

"Good luck. Dougherty out."

The admiral's image vanished abruptly, replaced by the incandescent mother-of-pearl glow of the Briar Patch, leaving Picard to wonder: What agreement did Starfleet—or Dougherty himself—have with the Son'a that neither wanted the *Enterprise* to discover? And why were both worried about anyone else having contact with the planet?

On the shuttlecraft viewscreen, the marbled blue Ba'ku planet rotated lazily inside its gleaming rings. No wonder the Son'a were so intrigued by it; here was astounding beauty without a trace of artifice, Picard decided, as he sat at the shuttle's controls. Beside him, in the copilot's chair, Worf spoke, squinting at his readouts.

"Sensors are not picking up any ships coming from the surface."

"Transmit a wideband covariant signal," Picard ordered. "That'll get his attention."

Complying, Worf touched controls on his panel. "He might be using the planet's rings to mask his approach."

Picard checked the sensors again. "The metaphasic radiation in those rings is in a state of extreme flux. Steer clear of them, Mister Worf."

The two of them contemplated the planet in silence

for a time, checking and rechecking sensors, watching, waiting. Picard murmured in singsong to himself, to the hidden android: "Come out, come out, wherever you are . . ."

Worf's thick brows came together in puzzlement; he faced his captain. "Sir?"

"Hmm?" Picard shook off the sudden strong recollection of his childhood, of himself in a long-ago summertime, hiding behind a grapevine thick with green leaves, redolent with the winy fragrance of cabernet franc grapes, some of them crushed on the soft, loamy soil beneath his bare, purple-stained feet. "Oh, it's just something my mother used to—"

A deafening roar; the small craft pitched leeward. "Hold on," Picard shouted over the din, and worked the controls. The shuttle climbed sharply, evading another phaser blast which lit up the viewscreen, dazzling the captain's eyes.

"Open all frequencies," he ordered Worf; the Klingon acknowledged and complied before Picard could draw another breath to speak. "Data . . . This is Captain Picard. Please acknowledge."

A second's silence; then another blast lit up the viewscreen; on the sensors, a Federation scout vessel appeared, firing continuously, as it slipped free from a gas cloud.

Picard maneuvered wildly, too erratically for a logical android mind to predict, and managed to evade the bulk of the shots—but enough connected, slamming the shuttle about in space, to remind him of the mission's danger.

Data, he silently told the android, *when I was the Borg's pawn Locutus, you found me, helped me find my way home. How can I help you now?*

The shuttlecraft reeled at another ear-shattering blast; Picard kept his wits and lurched the shuttle seventy degrees aft, then did a full spiral maneuver. In the midst of it, Worf—looking somewhat green, despite Picard's reminders that looking steadily at the viewscreen might make him feel ill—interrupted, his tone one of desperate inspiration. "Sir, if we force a tachyon burst, it may force him to reset his shield harmonics. When he does, we could beam him out."

"Make it so," Picard ordered.

The Klingon worked a few controls at tactical; at once, both viewscreen and sensors confirmed success.

"Direct hit," Worf exulted. "He's resetting his shield harmonics."

"Beam him out!" Picard turned toward the small transporter pad while Worf, clutching the modified transporter in his right hand, did the same.

The transporter glowed, hummed . . . then flickered, and wheezed, unsuccessful. Worf frowned at his panel. "He's activated a transport inhibitor."

"Prepare to enter the atmosphere," the captain countered. "We'll use the ionospheric boundary to shake him."

Abruptly, he piloted the shuttle into a straight dive down into the ionosphere of the planet's daytime half; on the viewscreen, the dust clouds and debris of the Patch disappeared. The darkness of space paled, and the blue atmosphere of the sky below brightened. But the ride was a bumpy one; Picard worked furiously to keep the ship from shaking herself apart.

"Scanners are off-line!" Worf shouted through the din.

"Evasive maneuvers. Heading one-four-zero mark three-one . . ."

A lightning-brilliant blast that thundered in Picard's ears made the controls in his hands tremble. Then another. Another. Another . . .

Above their heads, a conduit spewed blue-tinged gas; Worf half-rose, worked to stop it. In the viewscreen, the Federation scout zoomed past against a blue backdrop of sky—so close, that Picard found himself staring into Data's blank golden eyes.

He saw no evil there, no malice or madness, only the mindless focus of an android carrying out its programming . . .

Picard pulled yet another evasive maneuver, muttering aloud to himself: "He can fly a ship, he anticipates tactical strategies, his brain is obviously functioning . . ." He paused, groping for inspiration as it neared. "We've seen how he responds to threats. I wonder how he'd respond to—"

His words were interrupted by yet another deafening blast. No time to explain further to Worf; the shuttle could withstand little more. He turned excitedly to the Klingon, who had fixed the leak. "Do you know Gilbert and Sullivan?"

Worf blinked, utterly failing to grasp the implication, and clearly at a loss as to why his captain would make social conversation at such a critical moment. "No, sir, I haven't had a chance to meet all the new crew members since I've been back—"

"They're *composers,* Worf, from the nineteenth century. Data was rehearsing a part in *H.M.S. Pinafore* before he left." And he sang an aria at the open comlink:

A British tar is a soaring soul,
As free as a mountain bird,
His energetic fist should be ready to resist
A dictatorial word . . .

A subroutine, of course—Data was operating off one errant program at the moment that insisted he "defend" himself against attackers. But if Picard could manage to distract him long enough with another familiar program . . .

He gave Worf a nod that commanded, *Join me!* The Klingon returned the silent command with a look of pure exasperation: he did not know the lyrics, of course. Picard's fingers flew over computer controls as he sang:

His nose should pant and his lip should curl,
His cheeks should flame and his brow should
furl . . .

And over the comlink, much to the captain's gratification, another voice joined in: Data's. Together, he and Picard finished the chorus.

His bosom should heave, and his heart should
glow,
And his fist be ready for a knock-down blow.

On the shuttle monitor, the lyrics began to scroll past, with a bouncing ball to keep time.

"Sing!" Picard commanded, and the Klingon joined in somewhat reluctantly, in a rich baritone:

His nose should pant and his lip should curl,
His cheeks should flame and his brow should
furl . . .

Picard felt a momentary surge of concern when he realized the android had grown silent; but then Data joined in once more, in full tenor:

His bosom should heave and his heart should
glow
And his fist be ready for a knock-down blow.

Picard glanced at the Klingon at the realization that the android had stopped firing. And from the com, Data continued singing:

His eyes should flash with an inborn fire,
His brow with scorn be wrung;
He never should bow down to a domineering
frown . . .

The captain grinned and in the same soft tone, told Worf: "Prepare the docking clamps." The Klingon obeyed as Picard sang, triumphant, with his android friend:

. . . Or the tang of a tyrant tongue . . .

His foot should stamp and his throat should
growl,
His hair should twirl and his face should scowl
His eyes should flash and his breast protrude,
And this should be his customary attitude.

As they sang, Worf retook his chair and the shuttle glided beneath the scout. Picard launched into a repetition of the same verse and felt his vessel shudder as the docking clamp attached itself to the scout. Abruptly, he was singing alone:

His foot should stamp and his throat should
growl,
His hair should twirl and his face should scowl . . .

The shuttle began to rock from side to side—gently first, then harder, until Picard was forced to cling to the console to keep from being thrown against the bulkhead.

"Sir," Worf shouted beside him, "inertial coupling is exceeding tolerance. If we don't release him, he may destroy both vessels."

"I'm not letting go of him," Picard said stubbornly—even as the shuttle, still clinging desperately to the bucking scout, began to go into a downward spin. Through the viewscreen, Picard saw the planet surface spiraling dizzily toward them.

"Warning," the computer intoned calmly. "Impact with surface in twenty seconds."

"Reroute emergency power to inertial dampers," Picard commanded.

Worf worked the controls, then looked pointedly up

at his captain. "The damping sequencer was damaged by phaser fire!"

"Transferring controls to manual." Picard punched the controls furiously—he had not come this far only to die with two dear friends—while the computer reminded them:

"Warning. Impact with surface in ten seconds."

Picard finished transferring the controls; *respond,* the captain ordered the ship silently, as if his will alone were enough to create a cushion between them all and death.

At last, the Klingon looked up, exultant. "Damping field established."

"Maximum power! Now, Mister Worf!"

The Klingon rose and moved swiftly to the docking hatch. The shuttle responded once again to the controls; Picard pulled it (and by virtue of the docking clamp, the scout as well) into a hard arc parallel to the surface, only a dozen or so meters away.

In the instant that Worf blew open the scout's hatch with a harmless compression blast from the tricorder, he recalled the dream of the Kolar beast, and the delicious craving for battle that had overtaken him. A shiver of it swept over him as the hatch thudded to the deck of the scout's interior; for that flickering millisecond he contemplated the exhilaration hand-to-hand combat with the android would bring.

There was no chance the Klingon would win, of course; but ah, what a glorious death that would be, at the hands of such a worthy foe. . . .

Worf shuddered, casting off the madness, and adjusted his modified tricorder to Data's actuation frequency . . .

. . . just in time to see Data turn from the scout's control panel to blankly regard his intruder. In his eyes, Worf detected not the faintest glimmer of recognition; at once, he aimed the tricorder directly at the android, pressed the control, and waited for Data to fall . . .

Data did not fall. Instead, he tilted his head with dispassionate curiosity, still holding Worf with that blank gaze . . .

. . . and lunged with feline ferocity, feline grace.

Worf's first, atavistic urge was to drop the tricorder and strike a battle pose; but against all instinct, he extended the tricorder toward the android and again pressed the control. Data was his friend; and it was Worf's duty to both his friend and to Captain Picard to return with both himself and the android intact.

Data sailed toward him—and in midair, the android's amber eyes went abruptly dull; his body froze, immobile, and dropped to the floor with the same lifeless *thud* as the hatch.

With a sigh of relief . . . and disappointment, Worf touched his combadge. "Captain. Commander Data is safely in custody."

And almost smiled as he heard the deep intake and release of Picard's gusting breath.

FIVE

☆

Retrieve Data, then get out, Dougherty had said; but the admiral had not specifically forbidden Picard to go to the planet surface—and Picard was determined to test the limits of Dougherty's patience.

According to the *Enterprise*'s sensor readings, the entire Starfleet mission group remained down on the planet surface, along with a handful of Son'a—but if there were any real danger to them, the admiral would certainly have beamed them up. The agrarian Ba'ku wielded no transporter beam inhibitors, no shields, nothing whatsoever that could have prevented such a move. And Son'a vessels were supposedly technological marvels, with the capacity to beam up the mission team en masse, with no one left behind to suffer the wrath of their captors.

Even now, Riker had reported, all on the planet surface appeared peaceful—and if the delicate negotiations Dougherty had mentioned were in fact occurring, both parties must have reached an impasse. No communications had taken place between planet surface and the Son'a vessel for the past hour.

Whitewash, Picard decided. Everything Matthew Dougherty had told him thus far had been whitewash—a pleasant exterior that hid something rotten, rather like the thick layer of cosmetics worn by the aged Son'a. The admiral had been far too nice when Picard had shown up unannounced in the Briar Patch; if there *had* been real environmental concerns, the Dougherty Picard knew would have chewed him up and spit him out, and noted it all on the captain's record. The real Dougherty would have beamed up his people the instant the Ba'ku discovered the duck blind.

Something was seriously amiss—something that Dougherty and the Son'a had no intention of revealing, something that the captain would have to discover on his own.

So it was that Picard, accompanied by an entourage of armed engineers, entered the Ba'ku village on foot. Crusher and Troi flanked him, and the three, like the engineers, kept their phasers drawn.

It was difficult, if not impossible, to keep a somber, even threatening expression upon one's face, Picard reflected, given the natural beauty of the surroundings—the air fresh, rich with oxygen, the sky bright with sunlight filtered through the branches of sweet-smelling trees, the distant mountains lavender-gray beside a silver river, the closer mountains russet iced with green. And the birdsong . . .

He felt the muscles holding in his abdomen, his spine, suddenly release and flow outward like ice melting in the sun, and recalled when he had last experienced such utter relaxation: in childhood, on holiday along the southern coast of France. Only then, the breeze had been more humid, and carried upon it the astringent scent of salt. He had been running along the water's edge, laughing at the pull of tide and dissolving sand as the waves retreated, and maman had been sitting beside him, smiling, her dark hair pinned up, save for one errant curl at the nape of her neck. . . .

Picard shook off the memory and the beginnings of a smile. They had made their way to a copse of trees within a wildflower-filled meadow; in the shade, the Ba'ku sat at handmade wooden tables, apparently enjoying a leisurely lunch. The perfumed breeze carried on it the sounds of laughter and conversation.

They appeared a handsome, healthy people: pale-eyed, brown-skinned from the sun, well-muscled from a lifestyle dependent on physical labor. All wore loose-fitting robes of handwoven cloth dyed in the colors of nature: indigo, beet, saffron.

Among them sat their alleged hostages, still dressed in Starfleet uniforms but definitely off duty, given the amount of laughter in the air. Some of them sat observing the children and trying unsuccessfully to keep up with an extremely sophisticated, challenging form of patty-cake. The others conversed happily with their gracious Ba'ku hosts, who seemed intent on refilling their plates and cups. A small group of Son'a sat off to one side, apparently uninterested in either eating or socializing.

Picard and his rescue team stopped and regarded the charming tableau in curious silence; the luncheon conversation faded away as the observed registered their observers.

The Ba'ku looked as perplexed as Picard felt; the "hostages" looked frankly disappointed.

At once, the heads of the mission rose and moved toward Picard—one Son'a, one Starfleet.

"Captain. Subahdar Gallatin, Son'a command." The Son'a, a small-framed male with notably regal bearing and a serious, matter-of-fact manner, gave Picard an acknowledging nod almost as natural as an Earth-born human's. So, this was Ahdar Ru'afo's second-in-command; but Gallatin lacked his ahdar's arrogance and flamboyance in dress.

"Lieutenant Curtis," the Terran female said, "attaché to Admiral Dougherty." Her manner was cheerful and direct; if the admiral were trying to hide something, it seemed his attaché was excluded from the secret.

Picard stepped forward so the two stood beside, not in front of, him; he kept his weapon trained on the nearest tableful of quizzical Ba'ku. He addressed them softly, from the side of his mouth: "Are you all right?"

Smiling as if both amused and surprised by the question, Lieutenant Curtis gestured at the natives. "We've been treated extremely well by these people." If she had been taken hostage, her captors had obviously forgotten to share that information with her.

Indeed, the Ba'ku made no move to interfere, merely watched and whispered among themselves about these new intruders. Picard and Troi lowered their weapons; the rest of the team kept their phasers aimed at the natives.

Already bored, the children unself-consciously resumed their android-fast patty-cake game. Deanna Troi watched, spellbound. She glanced sidewise at the captain, then returned to watching the Ba'ku children with a faint smile of admiration and wonder. "They have an incredible clarity of perception, Captain. I've never encountered a species with such mental discipline."

As she spoke, a small group of Ba'ku made its way toward them; by their demeanor, Picard judged them to be leaders—although none of them appeared to be older than forty. The tallest, a male, walked up to Picard and faced him with a direct, open expression and an air of friendliness.

"My name is Sojef, Captain." He was broad-shouldered and powerfully built; a second male and a female followed and silently flanked him on either side.

"Jean-Luc Picard," the captain responded, then pointed with his chin. "My officers, Doctor Crusher . . . and Counselor Troi."

Sojef favored them each with a look, then half turned toward the waiting feast. "Would you like something to eat?"

"No," Picard answered, "we're here to . . ." He faltered as he gestured at the mission group. ". . . 'rescue' them."

"As you wish," Sojef replied politely. "But I would ask you to disarm yourselves. This village is a sanctuary of life."

Picard glanced down at the phaser still clutched in his hand and measured the request. A ploy? Possibly, but . . . He studied the apparently sincere expressions of Sojef and his entourage, of the smiling Lieutenant Curtis and obviously content Starfleet personnel, of the aloof Son'a, of the children playing, oblivious to the grown-up conversation.

Unlikely, that they would place their own children in a dangerous situation—or that they would be able to terrorize so many Starfleet officers into giving such a convincing performance. Picard holstered his weapon, and heard the rest of his away team do the same. To Crusher and Troi, he said, "Prepare to transport the 'hostages' to the ship."

Crusher acknowledged with a glance. "They should be quarantined before joining the ship's population."

Picard gave a nod. The women moved off with Subahdar Gallatin and Lieutenant Curtis to arrange transport, and the *Enterprise* engineers left to disassemble the duck blind—leaving Picard alone with the Ba'ku leaders.

He turned back to Sojef with a wry smile; there was no point in trying to hide his embarrassment at drawing weapons on the Ba'ku. Amazing, really, that these ostensible primitives were reacting so calmly to all the recent, startling events; he would not have blamed them for wielding a few pitchforks and torches. "We were under the impression they were being held against their will."

A petite, small-boned woman beside Sojef took a defiant step forward. "It's not our custom to have guests here at all, let alone hold anyone against their will." There was no harshness in her tone—only strength, and in her star-pale eyes, a fire that made Picard draw in a silent, startled breath. Her sleeves had been rolled up to reveal lean but muscular arms.

Sojef spoke next. "The artificial life-form would not allow them to leave. He told us they were our enemies, and more would follow."

"Are *you* our enemy?" the woman asked point-blank. No hostility in her tone, no suspicion, only a demand to know.

"Anij . . ." Sojef murmured, admonishing her gently; clearly these two had known each other quite well for some time. But she ignored him, keeping her unwavering gaze on Picard.

For a moment, he was almost too overcome by that gaze to speak, as if he were a giddy schoolboy with a crush. *Good Lord, what is the matter with you, man? You're a captain—act like one.* He gathered himself at once and straightened his uniform. "My people have a strict policy of noninterference with other cultures. In fact, it's our Prime Directive."

Anij—such a lovely, exotic name—favored him with a withering smile. "Your directive apparently doesn't include spying on other cultures."

"If I were in your shoes, I'd feel the same way after what happened." Picard paused, carefully weighing each word in light of the culture's technological advancement—or rather, lack thereof. "The 'artificial life-form' is a member of my crew. Apparently, he became . . . ill . . ."

The younger male who flanked Sojef spoke for the first time. "There *did* seem to be a phase variance in his positronic matrix that we were unable to repair."

Picard's lower jaw dropped a few centimeters; for an instant, he stared speechless at the younger Ba'ku.

Anij's wry smile widened. "I believe the captain finds it hard to believe that we'd have any skills repairing a positronic device."

The ever-serious Sojef nodded. "Our technological abilities aren't apparent because we've chosen not to employ them in our daily lives. We believe when you create a machine to do the work of a person, you take something away from that person."

"But at one time," Anij added, tilting a sharp chin to look up at Picard with eyes that challenged, "we explored the galaxy just as you do."

"You have warp capability?" Picard murmured, even more astonished.

"Capability, yes." She lifted her face toward the sunlight and spread both arms as if to embrace her entire world. "But where can warp drive take us, except away from here?"

It was a question that, at any other time, Picard would deem foolish, shortsighted, preposterous; but at that precise instant, a scarlet hummingbird, like a red-winged jewel, appeared just behind her head, and dipped its beak into her sun-lightened curls.

Finding no nectar, it moved on—toward Picard, and for a heartbeat, no more, he felt upon his scalp the breeze generated by small, invisible wings, heard the soft, fleeting hum . . .

Behind them, he could hear the affectionate murmurs of Starfleet personnel taking leave of their Ba'ku hosts. With sincerity, he told Anij: "I apologize for our intrusion."

And he took his leave of them—quickly, before further contact with Anij, the Ba'ku woman, made it any harder for him to go.

". . . and because they have warp capabilities, the consequences to their society are minimal," Picard finished. He sat in his ready room, staring at the image of Admiral Dougherty on the monitor. It had all gone precisely as he expected: Dougherty had not rebuked him for "rescuing" the "hostages" on his own initiative. Far from it: he had listened approvingly to the captain's tale, and had appeared surprised to hear of the Ba'ku's hospitality and their technological abilities.

Picard believed none of it.

Even now, Dougherty nodded, smiling with an enthusiasm that seemed a little too forced. "You've done a terrific job, Jean-Luc. Now, pack your bags and get the hell out of there."

Obviously, Picard thought, *I failed to find whatever he was hiding from me, or he wouldn't be so damned cheerful.*

Abruptly, the admiral's tone shifted, became both more genuine and concerned. "How's Data?"

"In stasis," Picard replied, trying not to be short, not to let any of the disbelief or disgust he felt toward Dougherty show. "La Forge is completing the diagnostic."

The admiral gave a compassionate nod; then his expression shifted once again to the brisk, the businesslike, the feigned. "I'll need all your paperwork tomorrow. We're heading back your way. Set a course to rendezvous with us so you can transfer the crew and equipment on your way out."

"You're not finished here?" Picard took care to keep his tone polite, disinterested, despite his suspicion. So, whatever the admiral wanted was still on the surface itself, and was not contained within the mission crew, their belongings, or the disassembled duck blind, all of which were now aboard the *Enterprise.*

"Just a few loose ends to tie up," Dougherty said casually, with a slightly too-big smile. "Dougherty out."

Picard touched a control; the monitor darkened, and he turned from it with a sigh. It was time to immerse himself once again in the myriad of annoying little missions Starfleet had planned for the *Enterprise* once she emerged from the Briar Patch, and he picked up one padd from a stack of them on his desk and began to study it.

He'd intended to read it with part of his mind while delegating another part to subconscious rumination about Dougherty's hidden agenda—if, indeed, he could be certain the admiral had one. He prided himself on his ability to work on two projects at once, so long as one was strategy and the other detail.

But at the moment, he seemed able to concentrate on neither. Instead, his gaze was drawn toward the observation window, where the beautiful planet of the Ba'ku, wearing its rings like opalescent jewels, rotated.

And he thought only of Anij; Anij, with her cool voice and fiery eyes, wearing the crimson humming-bird like an adornment in her hair . . .

At the same instant, Deanna Troi sat on her office couch making notes on a padd—or at least, trying to. Her concentration was definitely off—had been, since that incident with Will Riker in the library. She had flirted with him mercilessly as a schoolgirl, and had enjoyed it. Why?

Only one answer would come: *Because I wanted to.*

But *why* did she want to? She and Will had long ago

agreed to keep old feelings just that—*old* feelings—so why was she now in the throes of what felt like an adolescent crush?

Counselor, counsel thyself.

All right, then: she had acted irresponsibly with Will, had flirted with him because—because, well, she had been attracted to him. And it seemed to her that he had enjoyed the attention. Perhaps it had been only a game to him; perhaps it had been only a game to *her.*

Okay, it *had* been a game to her, a deliciously fun one. She had adored flirting with him when they were lovers, because he was sly and sharp-witted and had always caught on immediately to the subtlest innuendo. And he was a master at the game himself, especially at telegraphing the most erotic proposals at public social situations without another soul suspecting. (*Never* on duty, of course—nor would she have permitted it.)

But beneath the flirtatious game, she felt something deeper in herself—a real stirring of emotions she'd thought long gone, and that was a problem, especially if Will thought she had only been joking—

For gods' sake, Deanna, shut up! Stop thinking about yourself, and start behaving like a ship's counselor.

She drew in a deep breath and studied her padd again, with its list of new assignees to the *Enterprise,* scheduled for pickup the coming week. There were archeologists, of course, who were accustomed to starship transport and would have little trouble adjusting—but there were a handful of first-time Starfleet ensigns from various cultural backgrounds and planets who would require orientation and a bit of hand-holding until the first wave of homesickness wore off . . .

The door chimed. "Come in," she said, barely glancing up from her padd—

—and narrowly avoiding a double take at the sight of Will, smiling a bit sheepishly. Her pulse immediately quickened at a rush of pure adrenaline (much to her chagrin), but with consummate self-control, she managed a cool, "Hi."

As if he were not the one person in the universe she most wanted to see; as if she did not want to leap immediately into his arms.

The hell with maturity, she thought with sudden, mischievous vehemence. Something wonderful was happening between them; she would enjoy it, would play it to the hilt. The game was afoot: she had last been pursuer, he the pursued. Now it was time to switch roles.

"Got a minute?" he asked, a little awkwardly. "I . . . need a little counseling." She looked askance at him, and he shrugged; a bit of the old playful Will crept into his tone. "First time for everything." He glanced about the room, looking for a place to sit. "Do I . . . lie down . . . or what?"

It was the smooth, unctuous way he said *lie down* that was the signal flirtation had officially begun. Deanna pretended to miss it—why not make him work a little harder?—but inwardly, she smiled. In her most professional counselor's tone, she answered: "Whatever makes you comfortable."

He lay down, all right . . . with his head in her lap, and gazed up at her with a look of pure desire.

"This isn't one of the usual therapeutic postures," Troi said coolly, fighting the desire to stroke his hair, to lean down for a kiss. . . .

Will grinned wolfishly. "But it's comfortable."

Ah, she had him quite desperate now; primly, she said, "Why don't you try sitting up?"

"Why don't you try lying down?"

She feigned a sharp, exasperated breath, but could no longer entirely repress the grin that played at the corners of her lips. "You're in quite a mood today."

He sat . . . and kissed her, swiftly, holding back from a longer kiss, just in case he had misread her smile. She rose and pretended to be shocked. "Do you really need counseling, or did you come down here to play?"

Riker rose as well, matching her step for step: she took one step back, he took one step forward, toward her.

"Both," he said, quite seriously; she blinked in honest surprise. "I think I'm having a midlife crisis . . ."

"I believe you." She retreated again; he followed. The look in his eyes was one of such pure, heated desperation that she at once rejoiced and quailed. So, he felt as she did—passionately in love—but did they know what they were doing? Was this wise?

Ah, the hell with it. . . .

"I'm not sleeping well," Riker breathed, advancing.

"Doctor Crusher has something that'll take care of that. . . ." She retreated two steps more, then stopped, and watched him slowly move nearer, nearer. . . .

"What I need, I can't get from Doctor Crusher. . . ." He hovered, his face mere inches above hers; she could feel his breath upon her skin as he asked:

"Counselor, do you think it's possible for two people to go back in time to fix a mistake they've made?"

"On this ship," she said, in a voice so coy, so beckoning, that he flashed a full grin and looked exactly as he had twenty years before, "anything's possible."

Slowly, slowly, he brought his lips down to hers, and they kissed—

"Augh." Deanna shivered, repulsed by the sensation of a thousand tiny beetle legs crawling upon her cheeks, and pushed him away.

"Augh?" Will repeated, aghast.

"I never kissed you with a beard before." Massaging her offended skin, she gathered the confused Riker up and shoved him out the door.

He stood in the doorway, arms spread, palms face-out in a gesture of total disbelief. "I kiss you and you say *augh?"*

She pressed the panel and watched the door slide over his pathetic, tortured expression, through some miracle of will managing to keep from smiling until it was completely closed.

SIX

"I had to reconstruct Data's neural net and replace these," Geordi La Forge told the captain, as the two of them made their way down the corridors of engineering. "They contain memory engrams."

With great interest, Picard studied the pieces of gouged, scorched circuitry in La Forge's palm. The instant Geordi had called, the captain put aside all thoughts of the Edenlike Ba'ku planet and Anij and focused on the issue of Data. La Forge had promised to share some extremely interesting—and sensitive—information. "How were they damaged?" the captain asked.

"By a Son'a weapon," La Forge stated firmly, and at Picard's swift, sharp look, added: "There's no doubt about it, sir. *That's* what made Data malfunction."

Picard considered this, then said cautiously, "The Son'a reports claim they didn't fire until *after* he malfunctioned."

La Forge was unmoved; he squared his dark shoulders. "I don't believe it happened that way."

The chief engineer was not one to make hasty judgments; only hard, irrefutable evidence could prompt him to make such a pronouncement. Convinced, Picard took the step to the next logical conclusion. "Why would they fire at him without provocation?"

La Forge briefly put his fingers to his dark brow, as if to massage away a headache, then repressed the gesture and shrugged. Picard noted the move simply because La Forge seemed to be the only crew member lately who was not in exuberant spirits— captain included. Not that Geordi was in a bad mood, but that he seemed somewhat distracted, irritated.

"All I know is that he was functioning normally until he was shot," La Forge said—squinting, or was that merely Picard's imagination? "Then his fail-safe system was activated."

"Fail-safe?" It was the first time Picard had heard of it.

"His ethical and moral subroutines took over all his basic functions."

"So," Picard reasoned, "you're saying he still knew the difference between right and wrong."

La Forge confirmed with a nod. "In a sense, that's *all* he knew. The system is designed to protect him against anyone who might try to take advantage of his memory loss."

"And yet he attacked *us,*" Picard mused. "And told the Ba'ku we were a threat. . . ." *Dougherty knows why,* he thought, though, of course, he could not imagine the admiral actually approving of the act. Somehow, this had to do with Dougherty and the unpleasant Ahdar Ru'afo. But instinct did not constitute proof; Picard forced himself to negate the thought and keep an open mind.

He paused alongside La Forge as the engineer stopped at a closed panel, sealed off with security codes. Normally, Geordi was able to get past such devices with the ease of a virtuoso practicing scales— but today, he blinked down at them and actually squinted in an effort to see.

"Implants bothering you?" Picard asked.

He shook his head, of course; Geordi was always last to admit to any physical complaint. "I'm all right. I think I'm just tired."

The panel slid open, revealing a deactivated Data

serenely mounted in a diagnostic device attached to the bulkhead. La Forge touched a control; immediately, the android's eyes sprang open. For an instant, they were perfectly blank, and Picard experienced an instant of horror: was their friend beyond rescue?

Then the amber eyes softened with recognition, and Picard smiled at the android.

"Geordi?" Data asked, disoriented. "Captain . . . ?"

"You're on the *Enterprise,* Data," Picard said gently.

Data considered this, then paused, half lowering his eyelids, as he ran a self-check. "I seem to be missing several memory engrams."

Geordi opened his palm to reveal the scorched circuits.

"Oh," Data said matter-of-factly. "There they are."

Picard took a step nearer. "What's the last thing you remember?"

Again, the android half lowered his eyelids, then drew in a deep breath and sang.

His nose should pant and his lip should curl . . .

"From the mission," Picard corrected dryly.

"I was in an isolation suit collecting physiometric

data on Ba'ku children," Data responded. "My last memory is going into the hills, following a boy . . ."

And a handsome child he was, Picard thought, as he and Data followed Sojef to the copse of shade trees, where the boy, Sojef's son, sat playing with a small wriggly toy wound about his fingers. Artim was his name—after one of the songbirds, Sojef had explained—and he looked to be a year or so away from the onset of puberty, with sky-colored eyes and sun-kissed hair and skin. As Picard neared, he saw the toy in the child's hands was not a toy at all—but a brown creature that squirmed and slithered about the child's fingers like a cross between a tiny caterpillar and a seal.

As the group of adults approached, Artim scrambled to his feet, taking care not to harm his pet. At first he seemed cheerful enough—then blanched with sudden fear as he recognized Data. The android noticed it, of course; a small, vertical crease appeared on the pale golden brow . . . and Picard was not sure which of the two he felt sorrier for.

"Artim," Sojef said, without introducing the others, "do you remember where you were on the Day of Lightning, when the artificial life-form appeared to us?"

"In the hills," Artim answered, his blue eyes owlish as he glanced from his father to the android; he held his squirming pet as far as possible from Data, as if frightened the android might suddenly attack it. "By the dam."

Picard leaned down to the boy's height and asked gently, "Can you show us?"

In reply, Artim slipped his pet into his pocket and began moving toward the mountains. By that time, a small group of Ba'ku had gathered about them—*the smaller the town, the fewer the secrets,* Picard reflected wryly—and followed curiously.

It did not escape his attention that the woman Anij was among them. He had come to find out why the Son'a had attacked his friend, and had no intention of losing his focus . . . but if fate should bring her his way during the investigation, he would not resist. As they walked, he gazed at her, openly inviting her to join him . . . and to his delight, she did.

Her welcome, however, left something to be desired.

"Haven't you disrupted our lives enough?" Painfully candid, she was—but he would have it no other way; and this time, there was gentleness with the honesty.

"I understand how you feel," he answered simply. "I just want to retrace Data's movements, that's all."

"Why?"

He almost answered truthfully, then caught himself. It would be foolish to make statements about the

Son'a until he was absolutely certain as to the exact circumstances of what had happened. He broke off eye contact, though he still felt her gaze—pale, direct, fearless—upon him. "I don't like to leave questions unanswered."

"Then you must spend your life answering questions," she replied evenly, and increased her pace, leaving him behind.

Nor did she bother to look back; Picard allowed himself a brief, admiring glance at her, then returned his attention to Artim, who as he walked kept glancing fearfully up at Data.

"There is no need to fear me," Data responded, his tone soothing, his shimmering gold features aligned into the friendliest possible expression—though Picard saw the distress in the android's eyes. "I am operating within normal parameters now."

"What?" Artim frowned suspiciously up at him.

"They fixed me." Data smiled down at the lad, which only made Artim recoil further.

Sojef intervened. Before Data could say anything further, the Ba'ku leader stepped between his son and the android and put a protective hand upon Artim's shoulder. With surprisingly cool condescension, he cast a withering smile at Data and steered the child away.

Crestfallen, the android moved alongside Picard.

"The boy is . . . *afraid* of me, Sir."

"It's nothing personal, Data." The captain made his tone as soothing as possible—but it was clear words alone could not comfort the android. "You have to remember, these people have rejected technology."

Data released a sorrowful sigh. "And I am the personification of everything they have rejected."

Picard nodded in reluctant agreement. "Until this week, that young man probably never saw a machine, let alone one that walks and talks."

The android's expression turned rueful. "I do not believe I made a very good first impression." And he gazed pathetically at the child, who at the same time happened to look over his shoulder at Data—then, at meeting the android's glance, averted his eyes.

Artim led the group up into the rocky foothills; the mild exercise invigorated Picard. The expanding vista of meadow and town, river and mountains, ablaze here and there with intensely colorful, fragrant flowers, intoxicated him. *Spring fever,* he told himself. Spring fever it was, that made him want to burst into a sprint, seize Anij's elbow, and drag her, laughing and running, to the brook the group was nearing, and pull her in with him. . . .

But he was a starship captain with a serious mission; he censored the thought immediately, clearing his throat at the same time with a vehemence that prompted a glance from Data.

At last they arrived at the softly gurgling brook. The group held back to let Artim cross first; with the unself-conscious abandon of a child, the lad hopped on one foot across the stepping-stones in the moving water. Impulsively, Picard followed suit, marveling at the act's ease, at the sudden lightness of his feet. It was not until he reached the other side that he saw Data's curious expression, and the small, odd glance Anij directed at Sojef; at once, he collected himself, adjusted his jacket.

Lightness of heart or not, he had come to investigate. And so he watched somberly as the others crossed in adult fashion, walked somberly until the group made its way over a rise, and Artim pointed at a distant spot near a trio of boulders:

"I saw the first bolt of lightning over there. . . ."

Will Riker forced himself not to wince as the blade of the razor flashed, moving toward him in a graceful gleaming arc. Had the hand that wielded it been his own, he would have been even more nervous as it connected first with the cream-swathed hair of his beard, then with the tender skin of his chin; but the hand was Deanna's, and her touch was swift, delicate, sure.

And sensual. Will sighed deliciously, deliriously, as she—bubble-and-water-hidden siren, glorious cascades of hair pinned atop her head—withdrew the blade with a flourish, flicking it clean. For the first time in a very long time, he felt the coolness of air directly on that particular patch of skin. The rest of him—except for his head, naturally—was currently submerged in a private sea of divinely warm water and jasmine-scented bubbles.

Private, except for Deanna, of course, and her flashing blade: that had been the agreement. First, the removal of the beard, and then . . .

It was madness, of course; the madness of love, which at the moment made perfect sense. *Why*, Will wondered, shivering at the sweet, sharp sting of the blade, *have we denied ourselves this joy for so long?* Now *that* was crazy. . . .

"Bridge to Riker."

Worf's deep bass invaded the moment. Deanna instinctively dipped lower into the tub, hiding shining shoulders beneath a floating mountain of rainbow-reflecting bubbles, leaving only her siren's grin and the straightedge blade atop the surface.

Riker groaned inwardly. "Can I get back to you, Worf?"

The Klingon's tone was sympathetic but circumspect, as if he sensed rather than saw Will's predicament. "Admiral Dougherty's on the comlink, sir."

Riker let go a sigh of infinite frustration, and sat up straight, into a more professional position; immediately, the muscles of his abdomen and spine tensed. "Patch him through," he ordered, yielding, and fought the urge to scratch at the foamy soap bubbles that clung to his chest hair and tickled as they slowly popped. Beside him, Deanna's expression went from gleeful to glum; she set down the blade and settled against the side of the tub, careful not to cause any audible splashing.

This had better be good, Riker thought as the computer bleeped softly at him; but he forced a pleasant tone. "Yes, Admiral?"

Riker had had few dealings with Dougherty, but from them (and from what he'd heard from the captain), he expected to hear a cordial, pleasant tone.

He heard anything but; the voice that came over the com was harsh, impatient. "Why haven't you left orbit yet?"

In the periphery of his vision, Riker caught Deanna's look of surprise; he managed to mask his own, and answer smoothly, "Captain Picard is still on the surface, sir."

"Doing what?"

Dougherty's increasing irritation only served to spark Riker's determination to remain uncowed; perhaps it was stubbornness, perhaps professionalism, but Riker made his tone deliberately calmer. "He didn't want to leave until we could adequately explain why Data malfunctioned. Data's future in Starfleet could depend on it."

A lengthy pause as the admiral considered this; then Dougherty snapped, "Remind the captain his twelve hours are up."

"Yes, sir," Riker responded impassively.

"Dougherty out."

Will turned at once to Deanna; they shared a grim look.

"Something's rotten in paradise," she said; a few damp, errant strands of hair clung to her neck and shoulders. The humid mist above the water had brought a youthful flush to her cheeks, a brightness to her eyes. Beautiful as she was dry, Will decided, she looked even better wet. "Why is Dougherty so desperate for us to leave, when his own people have been exposed on the planet surface for much longer?"

"I only know one thing for certain," Riker said, with mock seriousness, as though he were about to share a startling revelation about the admiral. Deanna moved to him, bringing a small wave of water as she put her hands upon his shoulders, her gaze expectant, curious; she fell for it, of course; she always did.

"I can't report for duty like this," Riker finished—indicating, of course, the large swath of beard missing from his chin.

"I can fix that quickly enough," she said slyly, and seized the razor, flicking it so that it made an unsettling swoosh as it sliced through the air.

Riker gave a small yelp of delight, and dove beneath the water.

Inside the Son'a body facility, Dougherty turned away from the companel to observe Ru'afo, undergoing yet another cosmetic procedure—this one more medical in nature. As the Son'a reclined, eyes closed, a male medic lanced the ugly boils on his neck with a long syringe, which regularly filled with a disgusting-looking substance the color and texture of algae.

"Your body is producing far too many toxins," the medic was saying softly. "We've reached the limit of genetic manipulation. . . ."

Ru'afo's small eyes opened with the languor of a sunning reptile; but the pointed look he directed at Dougherty was far from mellow. "I won't *need* any more genetic manipulation if our Federation friends allow us to *complete* this mission."

Dougherty looked away, cursing silently; he had hoped the Son'a hadn't heard the conversation. From the beginning, Ru'afo had been furious at Picard's interference, had insisted the admiral order the *Enterprise* away; but Dougherty was unaccustomed to taking orders, much less those of a walking cadaver. Besides, he had explained to Ru'afo, it would stir up far more curiosity on Picard's behalf—curiosity that might cause the captain to contact command for verification—were he, Dougherty, to give an uncharacteristically harsh, unexplained order.

But Picard had not simply collected his android and gone home, as the admiral had fervently wished; instead, the captain kept pushing. And if he pushed much further . . .

In truth, Dougherty had no idea what he would do: he could no more harm Jean-Luc than he could break his promise to his dead wife, his beloved Madalyn. The question was, how long could he keep Picard out of harm's way . . . ?

Along with the Ba'ku, Picard and Data had made their way down the hillside toward a primitive earthen dam and neighboring lake—the exact area where Artim claimed to have seen the first blast of the strange "lightning." Thus far, Picard had seen nothing unusual—except, of course, for the landscape's haunting beauty. Colors were more vibrant here: the russets of earth richer, the meadow greens deeper, the floral reds and violets more dazzling, the blues of sky and water more intense. Even the air was sweeter than any he had ever drawn into his lungs; all of it filled him with an extraordinary sense of exhilaration. An hour on the planet surface felt like the equivalent of a months-long vacation; he felt younger, clearer, refreshed.

Beside him, Data frowned down at the tricorder. "Tricorder functions are limited due to heavy deposits of kelbonite in these hills," the android reported somberly, unmoved by the beauty surrounding him; if anything, he seemed mildly troubled by Artim and Sojef's rejection.

Picard reined in his thoughts and focused on the business at hand. "How about a passive radiation scan?"

Data at once adjusted his tricorder, then quizzically drew back his head, tucking his chin, at the readout. "Curious. There appear to be strong neutrino emissions coming from the lake."

Picard felt a surge of vindication . . . and disappointment. Vindication, because he had instinctively known there *was* something hidden here, some secret to be discovered; disappointment, because he had never wanted to learn for certain that Matthew Dougherty was a liar. Emotions warring within him, he watched as the tricorder readings led Data to the edge of the lake, then into ankle-deep water. . . .

Deeper and deeper, until, as the astonished Ba'ku murmured in surprise, Data walked straight into the lake and disappeared beneath the water. It parted before him, then covered the top of his head and swirled a moment before settling glassy smooth.

Nearby, Artim gasped, and moved over to Picard. "Can he breathe under water?"

"Data doesn't breathe," Picard replied matter-of-factly.

At the captain's utter lack of dismay, the boy calmed a bit and gazed back at the still surface of the water for an instant. Sojef moved alongside him, hovering protectively as if to shield him from the very idea the android represented. Not even noticing his father's presence, Artim persisted. "Won't he rust?"

Picard smiled to himself. "No."

An expectant hush fell over the Ba'ku as they waited. Alongside the child, Picard silently watched the glittering play of sunlight on the turquoise water where Data had disappeared. With a graceful swoop of dark wings, a long-legged waterfowl landed and sailed on the very spot.

A moment later, a large ripple appeared at the lake's far side, and Data's head emerged—then shoulders, torso, legs, until he at last stood on the other shore, drenched and dripping. "Sir," he called, moving purposefully toward the dam, "I believe I know what is causing the neutrino emissions. . . ."

And he climbed to the dam's top, to a great iron

wheel whose circumference equaled his height. Two strong Ba'ku, perhaps three, were needed to move it; but Data turned it easily, opening a floodgate that emptied the lake.

Fascinated by the display of strength, Artim watched with intense, innocent curiosity. "Are there other machines like him in the offland?"

Up to that point, Sojef had maintained a polite, if distant, demeanor; now he started, stung, as if the boy had slapped him. "The offland is no concern of yours," he countered—hotly at first, then cooling as he registered Picard's intrigued gaze upon him.

The water continued to rush out of the deep lake with a roar; as it did, the remaining water was oddly displaced by air—or what appeared to be nothing but empty air, but within a matter of several seconds, it became clear that *something* was there, something large and oblong. One of the dark waterfowl fluttered overhead, then landed upon the top of the invisible structure, a sight that made the Ba'ku surrender a collective gasp. Another duck blind, Picard at first thought, but as the lake drained further, spilling off the sides of the object, the shape became unmistakable.

A ship.

The still-dripping Data rejoined him. "The vessel is clearly Federation in origin, Captain."

" 'Just a few loose ends to clear up,' " Picard quoted

bitterly. What possible reason would Admiral Dougherty have for hiding a large cloaked ship—a transport one-third the size of the *Enterprise*—in the Ba'ku lake?

Determined to find the answer, he headed for one of the rowboats on the shore; Data followed. Artim attempted to follow, but his father clamped a hand on his shoulder.

"We're not interested in such things," Sojef told the boy firmly; at that same instant, Anij appeared and gave the Ba'ku leader a contrary look.

"*I* am," she said, and before Picard could push off from the shore, she hopped on board.

He could not deny that he was glad to have her accompany them, despite the fact that her reason for doing so was distrust; at the same time, there was no predicting what type of reception the ship's inhabitants, if any, would give them. "It might be wiser for you to stay on shore," he said.

She responded by grabbing an oar and pushing the small boat into the water.

Picard's reactions were two: the first, indignation, that she should so blatantly ignore an order—*no, not an order,* he reminded himself swiftly. *A suggestion.* She was, after all, a civilian, and this was *her* world, not his; she had a right to investigate any threat to her people. His second reaction was to suppress a smile of admiration as he watched the lean, well-defined muscles of her arms and shoulders working beneath her tanned skin as she rowed: this person knew what she wanted and did not hesitate to make it known. She'd be perfect for command. . . .

He seized the oar from her and began to row himself, toward the invisible ship; it did not take long before they arrived at the edge of the invisible vessel. Data pressed a sequence of controls on the tricorder; there came a loud metallic click, then a hum. And in the midst of the air, a slice of the ship's interior appeared—and grew, until the three of them stared into the entranceway, colored a familiar Federation taupe.

No security locks to prevent entry, Picard noted; these people were not expecting visitors.

He drew his phaser; beside him, Data did the same. The three of them climbed up into the hatch, and stepped inside . . .

. . . to the Ba'ku village, complete with market-place, meadow, and mountains. Anij gasped, her pale eyes wide.

Data glanced up from his tricorder readout. "It is a holographic projection." He stepped over to a gap in the illusion, where a sliver of metal hologrid showed through rockface. "Incomplete, I might add."

Picard leaned toward Anij's ear and said in a low voice, "What you're seeing is a computer-driven image created by photons and force fields."

Gaze still riveted on the illusory village, she murmured, "I know what a hologram is, Captain. The question is: why would someone want to create one of our village?"

Indeed. Picard considered the situation: Dougherty's evasiveness and desire for him to leave, Data's scorched memory engrams . . . He turned to the android. "Data, if you were following the children and discovered this ship . . ."

The android finished the thought. ". . . it is conceivable I was shot to protect the secret of its existence."

The captain nodded. "What possible purpose could a duplicate village have, except . . . to deceive the Ba'ku?"

Anij swiveled her head about and glanced at him sharply. "Deceive us?"

"To move you off this planet," Picard said. "You go to sleep one night in your village . . . wake up the next morning in this flying holodeck, transported en masse. Within a few days, you'd be relocated on a similar planet without ever realizing it."

Data tilted his head quizzically. "Why would the Federation or the Son'a wish to move the Ba'ku?"

Picard sighed. "I don't know. . . ."

The next instant, he was dazzled by a brilliant flash of plasma; it streaked past, close enough for him to feel its heat, smell the scent of ozone. The blast surged between him and Anij, struck the bulkhead behind them, dissolving rockface to reveal more of the metal grid. It ricocheted off, baptizing the three of them with skin-searing sparks. Data at once returned fire; Picard ducked, seized Anij, and shoved her out the hatch. She landed in the water outside with a loud splash, while Picard crouched in the hatch and himself began firing.

The exchange was intense, blinding; bit by bit, the holovillage grew pockmarked with metal grids, while Picard grew increasingly dazzled by the afterimage of the brilliant blasts. Many more, he knew, and he would be unable to see what he was firing at. . . .

At last, a figure—a male Son'a, the captain discerned, after much blinking to clear his vision—fell unconscious to the deck. The firing at once ceased.

"Computer," Picard ordered. "End program and decloak the vessel."

The computer obliged; Picard leaned out the hatch just as its silvery exterior appeared, reflecting sunlight off its bow.

Outside, Anij thrashed in the water, choking and coughing. At the sight of Picard, she shouted: "I can't swim!"

Picard—and Data, who had heard as well—dove promptly into the cold water; within a heartbeat, the captain reached for her, pulled her to him. She fought, flailing. . . .

"Don't panic," he said soothingly. She held on to his arms and calmed a bit, but looked up at his words, sunlight-pale eyes shooting sparks of indignation. Her short curls were dark, dripping; her coarsely woven clothes clung to her like a second skin, so that Picard could see the gooseflesh beneath.

"I've been shot at," she wheezed, "thrown into the lake out of an invisible ship that's come to abduct us all . . . what's there to panic about?" Yet despite the irritation and fear in her voice, he sensed a sly undercurrent of humor.

Data suddenly appeared in the water beside them. "In the event of a water landing," he stated pleasantly, "I have been designed to serve as a flotation device." He twisted his neck with a short, sharp motion; a series of soft clicks followed, and the android rose waist high above the surface, fully buoyant in the water.

If Anij shared any of her people's disdain for artificial life-forms, she failed to show it at that instant; instead, she clung gratefully to the floating android while Picard swam over to retrieve the rowboat.

With each stroke, Picard grew more furious. Surely Matt Dougherty could not be willingly involved in deceiving an entire race; this had to be the Son'a's doing. Perhaps they were threatening the admiral, holding him hostage. . . .

Or so the captain hoped. At any rate, he was determined to find out. . . .

Picard was still wet and angry by the time he and Data materialized in the *Enterprise* transporter room. Worf met them; Picard barely glanced at the Klingon as he strode off the transporter pad toward the corridor.

"Did any of the hostages mention a cloaked ship during their debriefings?" Picard demanded.

The Klingon shook his head. "No, sir."

The captain stopped short and looked up at Worf. "Debrief them again." He turned to move away, then did a double take at the sight of a massively swollen red sore right on the tip of the Klingon's nose. "Have you been in a fight, Commander?"

Worf dropped his gaze, clearly humiliated. "No, sir. It is a *gorch.*"

Picard frowned. *"Gorch?"*

Data leaned over and whispered the translation in the captain's ear; Picard straightened, embarrassed for the Klingon's sake. "Oh. Well." He directed a weak, sickly smile at Worf. "It's hardly . . . noticeable."

Which was a lie as huge as the *gorch* itself, of course; refusing to acknowledge Data's deadpan gaze upon him, Picard hurried out into the corridor, with the unfortunate Worf in tow.

Riker was on the move toward them, prompting the captain's second double take. At first, Picard thought simply that Riker had somehow grown ten years younger in the past few hours . . . and it was true, his second-in-command *did* look younger, as if he'd just enjoyed several hours with a cosmetician. But it was more than that: Will was missing something, something vital . . .

Riker grinned at the reactions of his three fellow officers: even Data was staring openly at his freshly denuded cheeks and chin. "Smooth as an android's bottom, eh, Data?" Will joked.

The android blinked, amber eyes wide as he somberly digested the comparison. "I . . . beg your pardon, sir?"

But Riker didn't answer; instead, he directed all his attention to the captain as the four moved toward the nearest turbolift. "Admiral Dougherty wants to know why we haven't left yet."

Picard felt his expression grow stony. "We're not going anywhere." He stepped inside the door to the waiting turbolift; the others followed suit. "Deck five."

Meantime, Riker had finally gotten a good look at Worf, and asked casually, "You Klingons never do anything small, do you?"

Worf gave him a sidewise glance that spoke of death and daggers, but otherwise ignored Riker. To the captain, the Klingon said: "Doctor Crusher asked to talk to you when you returned."

In reply, Picard touched his comlink. "Picard to Crusher."

The doctor's voice immediately answered. "Captain, the Son'a hostages declined to be examined. I had them confined to quarters."

The news was less than surprising. "And our people?"

Beverly hesitated only long enough to take in a breath, but Picard recognized that little hesitation all too well. It meant the doctor had something unexpected to report. "They all have slightly elevated levels of endorphin production," Crusher said. "Probably the result of the environmental anomalies here."

Picard gave a nod, even though Beverly would never see it. His exceptional exhilaration while on the Ba'ku planet suddenly made sense. "Are they in any danger?"

Another little pause and intake of breath. "Not at all. They're fine . . . in fact, they're *better* than fine. Increased metabolism, high energy, improved muscle tone. We should all be so lucky."

"Very good, Doctor. Picard out."

The turbolift halted, opened; accompanied by his entourage, Picard stepped out and headed for his quarters. At the entrance, he paused and turned to the

Klingon. "Worf, don't release the Son'a officers until I've met with Ahdar Ru'afo."

Worf nodded. "Aye, sir."

Picard turned to enter his quarters, but before he did, he caught a glimpse of Data, running a finger along Riker's clean-shaven chin, and heard the android proclaim:

"No, sir, it is not. As smooth as an android's bottom. . . ."

The door snapped shut behind him, sealing off Riker's response. "Computer, music," Picard ordered—then cringed at the first notes of a grim Beethoven piece.

"No. Not that. Something else. Something . . . Latin."

"Please specify," the computer said pleasantly.

He scowled to himself an instant, then brightened as inspiration struck. "A mambo."

At once, the room filled with trilling and the festive sounds of Latin brass. Picard felt the muscles of his neck and shoulders ease, felt his hips begin to sway in rhythm; he smiled faintly. "That's more like it."

Still keeping time, he moved to the bathroom and began to unfasten his collar. It was still damp, and his skin cold and clammy; the uniforms definitely did not dry as well as the old ones. He really ought to tell—

The thought stalled midway as Picard finally registered what his sense of touch was telling him. He had pressed his hand to his throat to try to warm the coldness there. . . .

The collar had been loose.

The collar had been loose, because the skin of his neck—which a day or two ago had been wrinkled, sagging, causing Beverly to complain—was taut, firm. Young.

Young, as though during his day with the Ba'ku, he had aged in reverse five, ten years. Marveling, he ran a finger beneath his chin, and saw the impossible. As the mambo swelled in the background, Picard searched for the familiar wrinkles around his eyes, upon his brow. . . .

The newer ones, gone. The older, distinctly fainter . . .

He thought of the Son'a—aged, decrepit, a dying race—and at last understood.

Night on the planet of the Ba'ku: an indigo sky so bright with tens of thousands of stars that Picard barely registered the absence of a moon. He knocked upon the wooden door of a house sculpted from clay, rather like the adobe dwellings of the Navajo—certainly just like all the other homes built on the flood—resistant rise beyond the meadow.

But this one was different, because he knew who

lived in it. And when Anij opened the door and regarded him with stellar-pale eyes—eyes, Picard realized, that were beautiful not solely for their calm, determined strength, but also for their wisdom—he hesitated not an instant, but asked straight out.

"How old are you?"

SEVEN

"We came here from a solar system on the verge of annihilation," Sojef said, "where technology had created weapons that threatened to destroy all life." He paused to accept a steaming cup of liquid from his son, then gazed at the crackling hearth; firelight danced in his calm, somber eyes, reflected off the few streaks of silver in his hair. Picard sat beside him, on a comfortable chair fashioned from a dark native wood; though extremely simple in design, it had been wrought with artistry and elegance by carpenters long practiced at their skill.

In response to the captain's question, Anij had (with typical Ba'ku proclivity to do things in groups) summoned Sojef, as well as the younger leader known as Tournel. Although no one had formally introduced Anij as a leader, it was clear that the two men valued her opinion. She sat on a cushion facing the hearth, upturned face orange with fireglow, arms wrapped around her knees. She stared frankly at Picard, trying to gauge his reaction.

As for Artim, the boy returned to the large kettle hung from a spit over the fire, and began to ladle another cupful while his father continued:

"A small group of us set off to find a new home . . . a home that would be isolated from the threats of other worlds." He paused and glanced back at Picard with a small, sudden smile. "That was three hundred nine years ago."

Picard looked at him in awe. "You've not aged a day since then?" By all accounts, the man appeared to be in his early forties.

Sojef shrugged. "Actually, *I* was a good deal older when we arrived . . . in terms of my physical condition."

Anij unwrapped her arms and leaned forward. "There's an unusual metaphasic radiation coming from the planet's rings. It continuously regenerates our genetic structure. You must have noticed the effects by now."

Picard gave her a small, sheepish smile. "We've . . . just begun to." He took the cup proffered by Artim, and inhaled the steam: it smelled of pomegranates and flowers. He looked up at the boy and said wryly, "I suppose you're seventy-five."

Artim blinked at him, then with charming childlike candor said, "No. I'm twelve."

The adults smiled. "The metaphasic radiation won't begin to affect him until he reaches maturity," Tournel explained.

Picard took a sip of the hot liquid, apparently a type of fruit cider, and by any cultural standards delicious, with a perfect balance of sweet to tart. For a beat, he gathered his thoughts, then said: "To many offlanders, what you have here would be more valuable than gold-pressed latinum. And I'm afraid it's the reason that someone is trying to take this world away from you."

Artim's large eyes widened. "The artificial life-form was right?"

Picard gave a reluctant nod. "If not for Data, you'd probably have been relocated by now."

"How can we possibly defend ourselves?" Tournel asked.

Perhaps it had been a rhetorical question, perhaps not; in either case, Picard had no chance to reply. Sojef rose from his seat, and with sudden, startling vehemence, said: "The *moment* we pick up a weapon—we become one of *them*. We lose everything we are. . . ."

"It may not come to that," Picard countered swiftly. As the others turned to him, he added, "Clearly, the architects of this conspiracy have tried to keep it a secret. Not just from you, but from my people as well." He paused. "I don't intend to let them."

Outside, the air was redolent with the fragrance of night-blooming flowers; Picard and Anij strolled down the deserted main street, having escorted the others home. The danger at hand had been thoroughly discussed, strategy agreed upon; there was really nothing more to keep Picard from beaming back up to the ship. . . .

Only Anij. As she walked, she looked up at the stars, still twinkling in a sky that was lightening to lavender-gray in the predawn; in her eyes was a muted sorrow. "We've always known that to survive, we had to remain apart. It hasn't been easy. Many of the young people here want to know more about the offland; they're attracted to stories of a faster pace of life."

"Most of my people who live that faster pace would sell their souls to slow it down," Picard answered softly.

She looked over at him, her expression gently teasing. "But not you."

He smiled at her. "There are days . . ."

She studied him with a gaze so intense he almost flushed. "You don't live up to your reputation as an offlander, Picard."

He looked down, embarrassed by her frank admiration. "In defense of offlanders, there are many more like me . . ."

". . . who wouldn't be tempted by the promise of perpetual youth?" Her eyebrows and one corner of her mouth quirked skeptically upward. "I don't think so."

With a rush of sudden warmth to his cheeks, he *did* blush, something he hadn't done since a teenager; the fact clearly charmed her. "You give me more credit than I deserve," he said. "Of course, I'm tempted. Who wouldn't be? But . . . some of the darkest chapters in the history of my world have involved the forced relocation of a small group of people to satisfy the demands of a larger one. I'd like to believe we learn from our mistakes." He thought of Admiral Dougherty and sighed. "Obviously, some of us haven't."

He paused in midstride as they passed a courtyard; beneath an awning, an exquisitely handcrafted quilt was stretched out in a wooden frame.

"Extraordinary craftsmanship," he breathed, reaching out to touch it—then stopping himself, lest his fingers somehow mar its beauty.

Anij smiled with amusement. "That's the work of students." And at his amazed reaction, she added, "They're almost ready to become apprentices. In thirty or forty years, some of them will take their place among the artisans."

"*Apprenticing* for thirty years," Picard marveled, as they continued their stroll. "Did your people's mental discipline develop here?"

"More questions." Her eyes narrowed teasingly, and her expression became childlike, alive, full of the same impulsive playfulness that had overwhelmed Picard on his first visit here. He wanted to chase her, seize her, laugh aloud—but instinct held him back. "Always the explorer. If you stay long enough, that'll change."

"*Will* it?" he murmured, challenging her.

"You'll stop reviewing what happened yesterday, stop planning for tomorrow, until you find—" She broke off abruptly. "Let me ask *you* a question—have you ever experienced a perfect moment in time?"

He gazed at her, puzzled. "A *perfect* moment?"

She looked about, as if literally searching for the right words. "When time seemed to stop . . . and you could almost *live* in that moment. . . ."

He nodded enthusiastically, understanding, and smiled inwardly at the memory. "Seeing my home planet from space for the first time . . ."

In her excitement, she seized his wrist. "Yes, *ex-*

actly. Nothing more complicated than perception."
She paused, casually letting go of him as if not even
realizing the two of them had touched—though Picard had been exceptionally aware. *"You* explore the
universe. *We've* discovered a single moment in time
can be a universe in itself, full of powerful forces.
Most people aren't aware enough of the *now* to ever
notice them."

Her face glowed incandescent with an interior joy;
smitten by her passion, her youth, her age, her wisdom, Picard gazed at her with a gently rueful smile. "I
wish I could spare a few centuries to learn."

She laughed softly. "It took us centuries to learn
that it doesn't have to take centuries to learn."

They were at her door; as she turned to him to take
her leave, he said, with feigned seriousness, "There's
one thing I don't understand." And at her questioning
gaze, continued: "In three hundred years, you never
learned to *swim?"*

For once, he had her at a disadvantage; she grinned,
embarrassed. "I just . . . haven't gotten around to it
yet." She stepped onto the threshold, then paused and
turned in the doorway, the grin suddenly gone, her
tone gentle. "I wonder if you're aware of the trust you
engender, Jean-Luc Picard. In my experience, it's
unusual for . . ."

". . . an offlander?" he teased.

Her lips curved upward. "For someone so young."

And she gave him a look that was pure electricity; for an instant, all else in the universe vanished, and nothing existed for him save Anij, and her star-bright, depthless eyes. How was it possible, he wondered, that one so jewellike, so strong, so amazing and beautiful should be alone?

She turned away from him—too soon—and stepped over the threshold into her house, lit only by the dying fire; it took all of Picard's restraint not to call to her, not to follow, not to ask to stay.

Once inside, she glanced back over her shoulder at him and smiled, so dazzlingly that he drew in a breath; and then she was gone.

He could very well have beamed up at that instant—but he could not let go of the moment, not so quickly. Instead, he turned and walked out onto the empty street, through the quiet town, and watched the horizon brighten with a coral glow.

As he did, he noticed in the feeble light the solitary silhouette of a man also watching the encroaching dawn. He neared, and recognized one of his own.

"Geordi . . . ?"

La Forge turned . . . and Picard was momentarily struck dumb. Gone were the engineer's white optical implants; in their place were ordinary human eyes, with irises of soft, deep brown.

Geordi smiled at Picard's amazement. "Funniest thing, Captain. There wasn't anything wrong with my implants; there was something *right* with my eyes. When Doctor Crusher removed the ocular connections, she found the cells around my optic nerves—"

"—had regenerated," Picard finished for him.

La Forge nodded. "It may not last after we leave. If not, I just wanted, before we go . . ." Emotion crept into his tone; he cleared his throat, then continued evenly. "I've never seen a sunrise. At least, not the way you see them."

Picard considered this, then without a word, turned his attention back to the coming dawn. Geordi followed his gaze, and together they watched as first the sun's rays, and then the orange solar disk, peeked over the distant mountains. The sky gradually lightened from indigo to gray to lavender to coral and crimson; the lake glowed incarnadine, as if aflame. Slowly, the homes, the meadow, the square, began to lighten, from gray monochrome to the entire brilliant spectrum of color.

The air, chilly on Picard's face, began to warm; he felt renewed, reborn. He looked, smiling, to La Forge—then turned away again at the sight of a single crystalline tear sliding down Geordi's dark cheek.

In the ready room, Picard sat trying to concentrate on one of the padds taken from the stack spread out on his desk—the mundane clutter spawned by running a starship. His thoughts were elsewhere: on the

Ba'ku planet, and the two announced visitors bound to arrive any instant.

He had detained the Son'a officers for precisely that reason: to force Dougherty and Ru'afo to react, to come onto his, Picard's, turf for a confrontation.

The door slid open without chiming; Picard moved only his gaze upward, keeping his face downturned toward his work.

Ru'afo swept in a full step ahead of Dougherty. Against the backdrop of the *Enterprise*'s muted decor, the Son'a's costume seemed even more garish: crimson and aubergine brocade robes embroidered with latinum and embedded with black pearls, topped by a heavy latinum yoke studded with amethysts and rubies. Compared to the innocent, sun-kissed beauty of the Ba'ku, the ahdar was all artifice—a Halloween ghoul with kohl-shadowed eyes and a pallid, taut mask for a face.

A furious ghoul, at that; even the carefully applied powder on Ru'afo's cheeks could not hide the dark flush of anger there. While Dougherty stood a respectful distance from the captain, Ru'afo charged forward and leaned down, manicured hands gripping the edge so tightly that blue-green veins stood out in bas relief. A nauseating wave of cloyingly sweet perfume mixed with an undercurrent of decay emanated from his robes.

Picard studied the Son'a's hands briefly, then pretended to return his attention to the padd in front of him. It was an affront to ignore a higher-ranking officer, of course; a part of him wanted desperately for Dougherty to take offense, to demand to know the reason . . . to be surprised when Picard told him the truth. After all, Dougherty had not grown any younger since the Ba'ku mission; if anything, he seemed to have aged.

The logical part of Picard's mind, however, knew it could never happen; Dougherty's involvement was clear. Considering the recent loss of his wife, it was more understandable—but no less despicable.

"Am I to understand that you're not releasing my men, Captain?" Ru'afo thundered.

At last, the captain set the padd aside and fixed both men with a look. "We found the holoship," Picard said softly.

The Son'a immediately let go the desk and straightened; but his anger only increased—as if it were Picard who had committed the crime, and not he. He turned, furious, to Dougherty as if the admiral was also to blame.

Dougherty shifted uncomfortably, his gaze directed inward and clearly unhappy with what he saw there; at the same time, he was resolute. "Ru'afo," he said, in a low, even voice, "why don't you let the captain and me—"

"No!" the Son'a shrieked, his face contorting so

vehemently with rage that the tightly stretched scar on his forehead split open, leaving rills of blood in its wake. Oblivious, he ranted on. "This entire mission has been one Federation blunder after another. You will return my men, or this alliance will end with the destruction of your ship."

And with a darkly glittering swirl of robes, he left, leaving Dougherty and the captain to appraise each other silently. Picard could not entirely hide the disgust he felt.

Uncertainty and shame fled the admiral's expression, replaced by a cold defiance as Dougherty frankly studied Picard; after a measure, the admiral spoke.

"You're looking well, Jean-Luc. Rested."

"Your Briar Patch turned out to be more hospitable than I expected."

Dougherty gave a reserved nod. "That's why we put chromodynamic shields in place—so our people wouldn't feel the effects from the metaphasic radiation—"

"—or understand that they were participating in the outright *theft* of a world," Picard finished. "I won't let you move them, Admiral. I'll go to the Federation Council. . . ."

"I'm acting on *orders* from the Federation Council." A lie, Picard thought at first, but Dougherty's tone was heavy, flat, matter-of-fact, his gaze unwavering; he was telling the truth.

The captain drew in a startled breath, incredulous. "How can there be an order to *abandon* the Prime Directive?"

"The Prime Directive doesn't apply," Dougherty said, so easily and reasonably that he must have given the speech several times before. "These people are not indigenous to this planet. They were never meant to be immortal. We'll simply be restoring their natural evolution."

Picard stood, aghast, unable to believe that he was hearing such words from a Starfleet admiral's—much less Matthew Dougherty's—lips. "Who are *we* to decide the next course of evolution for these people?"

"There are *six hundred* people down there," Dougherty said, tensing; heat crept into his tone. "We'll be able to use the regenerative properties of this radiation to help *billions.*" He paused. "The Son'a have developed a procedure to collect the metaphasic particles from the planet's rings. . . ."

"A planet in *Federation* space," Picard reminded him.

"Right." Dougherty let go all pretense of civility; he moved in until only the desk separated the two men, his expression hard. Gesturing at the air, he said, *"We* have the planet, and *they* have the technology—a technology we can't duplicate. You know what that makes us? Partners."

Picard leaned forward with equal heat. "Our partners are no more than petty thugs."

Dougherty dismissed the notion with a wave. "On Earth, petroleum once turned petty thugs into world leaders. Warp drive transformed a bunch of Romulan thugs into an empire. We can handle the Son'a; I'm not worried about that. . . ."

Picard thought of the four nearby Son'a ships, each of them dwarfing the *Enterprise,* and said dryly, "Someone probably said the same thing about the Romulans a century ago."

"With metaphasics," the admiral continued, ignoring him, "lifespans will be doubled. An entire new medical science will evolve. . . ." He looked at Picard, his gaze one of hope mixed with a grief so profound that the captain almost took pity. "I understand your chief engineer has the use of his eyes for the first time in his life. Would you take that away from him?"

It was a difficult, if not impossible, question to answer; Picard thought of all the loved ones lost over so many years. His parents, grandparents, great-grandparents, might all still be alive this moment. Was it right to take from the Ba'ku to give to them?

There had to be another way. If the technology were possible, then a way could be found, and soon, without destroying a culture, a world. "There are metaphasic particles all over the Briar Patch," Picard reasoned. "Why does it have to be *this* planet?"

"The concentration in the rings is what makes the whole damned thing work," Dougherty interrupted. "Don't ask me to explain it. I only know they inject something into the rings that starts a thermolytic reaction. After it's over, the planet will be unlivable for generations."

"Delay the procedure," Picard said. "Let my people look at the technology."

Dougherty shook his head, with a heaviness that spoke of sleepless nights spent trying to solve the dilemma; light played on his silver hair. "Our best scientific minds already have. We can't find any other way to do this."

"Then the Son'a can establish a separate colony on this planet until we do."

"It would take *ten years* of normal exposure to begin to reverse their condition," Dougherty said. "Some of them won't survive that long. Besides, they don't want to live in the middle of the Briar Patch—who would?"

"The Ba'ku," Picard said softly. He shared a long look with Dougherty: clearly, the admiral would not yield—but the captain was bound to try. "We are betraying the very principles upon which the Federation was *founded;* this is an attack on the very soul of the Federation." He paused, remembering Anij in starlight, the quiet village streets, the sunrise. "This will destroy the Ba'ku. Just as cultures have been destroyed in every other forced relocation throughout history."

Dougherty sighed with pure exasperation. "Jean-Luc, we are only moving *six hundred* people."

"How many people does it take before it becomes wrong?" Picard asked him. "A thousand? Fifty thousand? A million? How many will it take, Admiral?"

Dougherty's expression and voice went cold; a veil had descended and could not be pierced. "I'm ordering you to the Goren system," he said, with a harshness Picard had never heard in him. "I'm also ordering the release of the Son'a officers. File whatever protests you wish to. By the time you do, this will all be done."

Then he was gone. Picard sat down heavily to contemplate not only the future of the Ba'ku . . . but his own.

And more. Something about Ru'afo's outburst had stirred in the captain an unpleasant memory, one which refused to surface at the moment. Picard suspected that the key to the Son'a lay buried in Ru'afo's anger and hatred—the timbre of which struck Picard as hauntingly familiar.

Yet, try as he might, he could not remember . . .

It was Riker, really, who noticed it first: something in the cant of Picard's head, his carriage, the peculiar intensity in his eyes as he stepped from his ready room onto the bridge. The captain was trying to hide it, of course—and usually was damned good at subterfuge; but Will had known him too many years, had seen him step down onto the bridge in just that way too many times.

Indeed, over the years he had noticed the barely perceptible slowing as Picard took that step—and, in the past few days, had seen the captain's pace quicken with the same youthful lightness Will himself felt. Now, however, there was gravity in Picard's step, a solemnity that weighed down every slightest movement.

Riker straightened in his seat at command, and in the periphery of his gaze, noticed that Data at ops and Worf at conn were both studying the captain with the same concern. Obviously, the Ba'ku had lost the battle, and whatever Dougherty and the Son'a were hiding was not illegal; if it were, the Son'a ships would be firing on them by now, and Picard would have already sent off the shuttle to carry word to Starfleet Command.

Yet there was something more amiss here, something Riker could not read. He waited patiently until Picard moved deliberately over to him and issued the quiet order:

"Prepare the ship for departure at oh-seven-hundred hours."

The commander did not reply, but waited expectantly for further explanation, which was surely forth-coming. He met the captain's gaze directly, silently asking; in response, Picard's manner was cool, veiled. He was hiding something from his second-in-command; and Will knew Jean-Luc well enough to realize there was only one reason the captain would ever keep information from his crew: to protect them.

"Aye, sir," Riker answered at last.

Picard turned away, his back toward Data, who shot a look at Riker; the android's golden eyes were frankly quizzical. Riker gave a faint, minimal shake of his head: he had no explanation to give. Instead, he watched along with the other crew members who knew the captain well, watched as Picard crossed slowly to the turbolift. Before entering it, the captain paused . . .

. . . and as subtly as possible, swept his gaze over the bridge.

Memorizing it, Riker realized with a flash of intuition. Imprinting it on his memory, because he never expected to see it again.

And in his quarters, Picard stood quietly a moment beside the table covered with star charts and padds, remnants of his research into the Briar Patch, the Ba'ku.

Others would find a way soon enough to replicate the Son'a's technology, given the recent discovery of

metaphasic radiation by Federation scientists. Give
the Vulcans a year or two, and they would find a way
that would not require the destruction of a planet, the
relocation of a people. Grief had clouded Dougherty's
mind; he was letting the Son'a influence him—and
they were desperate.

Dougherty had said as much himself: *It would take
ten years of normal exposure to begin to reverse their
condition. Some of them won't survive that long.*

So an entire world—a true paradise—would be
destroyed in order to accommodate the impatience of
criminals. A more peaceable solution could be found
in far less than ten years; surely the Son'a, with their
astounding technical skills, could develop one far
sooner. Why were they insisting on stealing and
destroying the Ba'ku planet?

Instinct told Picard there was something deeper
here, an answer hidden in the hatred in Ru'afo's eyes.

But Dougherty had finally called his, Picard's, bluff,
had issued direct orders: release the Son'a officers and
head for the Goren system. Picard had every intention of obeying the first order; Ru'afo seemed quite
capable of destroying the *Enterprise,* and the captain
would do nothing to endanger her.

Once the *Enterprise* was safely out of the Briar
Patch, however, the Son'a were no longer a threat . . .
and whatever Dougherty and the Son'a had told the
Federation Council, it had not been the whole truth.

The council members needed to understand more clearly what was happening. . . .

And Will Riker was just the man to explain it to them. Afterwards, he could obey Dougherty's order and head for the Goren system—unless, of course, the council saw fit to supersede the admiral's command.

Picard would remain behind, in direct violation of a superior's order—a court-martial offense. And so he slowly removed each pip from his uniform, setting the first one carefully atop his dresser; then the second, third, fourth . . .

Aboard the Son'a flagship, Subahdar Gallatin entered the body sculpture chamber and chided himself for his newfound perspective: after weeks among the Ba'ku, he was beginning to find the Son'a love of artifice offensive. It had been hard enough to watch the Ba'ku from the shelter of the duck blind; but after the android destroyed it, it had been even harder to sit among them, to see the joy they took in each other, in their children. To remember a way of life that called not for deceit, but trust. . . .

Gallatin passed by a cubicle and caught a glimpse of Natirim, the eldest Son'a, his mouth agape as a clinician implanted the last of a startlingly white set of teeth into his worn gums. Poor Natirim—he was so old, so worn that even the cosmeticians could not hide the signs of death's approach. With the last of his new teeth in, the old Son'a sat forward and smiled at himself in the mirror—a bright, gleaming smile set in aged, corrupt flesh. Natirim's complexion was cracked, scarred where the delicate skin had split from too many facial surgeries; beneath its surface, dark, mottled green boils festered—too many for the doctors to keep drained.

For Natirim, we do this, Gallatin reminded himself, even as the image of the Ba'ku meadow came unbidden to him, and the memory of its sweet fragrance. Who could say how much time the poor old fellow had left to him? One year? Ten?

At the same time, a different voice in his head whispered: *And what right have you to destroy this world?*

He censored the thought immediately with another: *Will I stand by idly and watch the first one of us die?* Impossible; he could never permit such an outrage. And yet . . . it had been difficult, on the planet surface, to hold on to the anger.

He moved quickly past the cubicles, until he arrived at the most private, luxurious one of all. There the ahdar sat, his head locked in a face-tautening frame; an Elloran cosmetician worked the device until it pulled Ru'afo's skin so tight, his closed eyelids slanted upward at an alarming diagonal. The recently erupted scar upon Ru'afo's forehead had already been resealed.

Gallatin came to a halt a step away from his commander, just as the Elloran woman gathered the loose skin at Ru'afo's left ear, and snipped it off neatly with a laser. As she did, Ru'afo sensed a presence and opened his eyes.

"Gallatin! So the righteous Starfleet captain finally released you. Did you encounter any problems on the surface?" The ahdar's tone smiled, even if his face—stretched far too tightly now—could not.

"No, sir." Gallatin hesitated, then came forth with the truth. "But it wasn't easy . . . being among them . . ."

"I'm sure," Ru'afo replied promptly, dismissing Gallatin's distress without an atom of empathy. It was Ru'afo who had masterminded the plan to extract revenge on the Ba'ku; Ru'afo who had always been the one in favor of violence, of lawlessness. "Just don't forget what they did to us. We'll have them rounded up in a day or two . . . we needn't bother with the Federation's holoship anymore. Just get the holding cells ready."

Gallatin acknowledged with a nod—at the same time, forcing himself to remember the day, long ago, when all of them had been given, in effect, a death sentence.

You're being more than kind enough, he told himself. *They sent you off to die. All you're doing is returning the favor.*

He turned and left, not before catching Ru'afo's words to the cosmetician: "I'm going to miss these little flesh-stretching sessions of ours, my dear."

Inside the cockpit of the captain's yacht, an out-of-uniform Picard worked the transporter controls and watched as several cases of military supplies materialized on the platform. That was worth a court-martial in itself—stealing Federation military supplies, not to speak of the way he intended to use them. . . .

He paused to study a translucent geological scan of the planet surface. Data had mentioned that the amount of kelbonite in the mountains had disrupted use of the tricorder. If that were so, then—

The android's voice emanated from behind Picard, as if the captain's very thoughts had summoned him.

"Rerouting the transport grid to avoid detection was wise," Data said, as Picard swung around to stare at him. "But the transporter is rarely used after oh-two hundred hours."

Beside the android stood Deanna Troi; Beverly Crusher; Geordi La Forge with his soft, dark eyes; Commander Worf; and Will Riker. All but Riker and La Forge were out of uniform; in a flash, Picard realized what was afoot—just as his senior crew had obviously inferred his intent.

Troi tilted her head and gave him a cat-caught-the-mouse smile. "Taking the captain's yacht out for a spin?"

Worf had already moved onto the transporter platform and was inspecting the cargo. "Seven metric tons of ultritium explosives, eight tetryon pulse launchers, ten isomagnetic disintegrators . . ."

"Looks like you're planning on doing some hunting," Riker said. His words carried a hint of humor, but his tone was all seriousness. Clearly, he had divined what his captain was about to do; Picard silently blessed—and cursed—him.

"Return to your quarters," Picard told them, taking care to keep voice and expression as cold and unyielding as possible. It was acceptable for him to risk courtmartial, but he would not permit his crew to do the same.

No one moved.

"That's an *order.*"

No one moved.

Will gave him a look as impenetrable as his own. "No uniform? No orders."

La Forge stepped forward. "Captain, how could I look at another sunrise, knowing what my sight cost these people?"

Picard had always fancied himself the most stubborn person in the galaxy; that was before he had worked with this particular crew. He sighed, yielding, and no longer tried to hide the gratitude he felt toward each of them. The change in his expression must have tipped them off immediately, for they all suddenly smiled, relieved.

Data interrupted the warmth of the moment. "I feel obliged to point out that the environmental anomalies may be stimulating certain rebellious instincts common to youth that could affect everyone's judgment." He paused. "Except mine, of course."

Crusher turned to him, only half serious. "Okay, Data, what do you think we should do?"

The android tilted his head, and studiously regarded each person in the group . . . then blinked, took a phaser rifle from the bulkhead rack, and activated it with lightning-swift grace. "Saddle up. Lock and load."

At that, the crew turned their attention back to the captain—awaiting instructions, Picard realized, with a welling of affection that tightened his throat. He collected himself, then said, "They won't begin the procedure while the planet is inhabited. So our job is to keep the planet inhabited." He looked to Riker and La Forge. "Will, Geordi . . . go back and put a face on what's happening here. Make the council see the

Ba'ku. It's too easy to turn a blind eye to the suffering of an unfamiliar people."

Riker acknowledged with a confident nod. "I'll be back before you know it."

Picard held his second-in-command's gaze a second longer; Will always faced danger with a cavalier attitude, but the captain's instinct—and his odd emotional understanding of Ru'afo—told him the *Enterprise* might very well not return. And Will was just as aware of the fact.

Softly, he told Riker: "We'll hold out for as long as we can."

EIGHT

Padd in hand, Gallatin strode into the tactical room, feeling the painful pull of a deep frown in his too-taut brow. The information on the padd had him concerned; he resented any interference in the Ba'ku project and had counted on it going swiftly, cleanly . . .

. . . in part, because he did not want to have to think about what the Son'a were doing here.

We're doing good. We're taking this incredible healing power not only for ourselves—who deserve it most of all—but for the entire galaxy. We're not even killing them—

It was Gallatin himself who had convinced Ru'afo that the Federation would swoop down hard on the Son'a. True, the Son'a had the advantage of better technology, but in terms of sheer numbers, they could not withstand an assault by the Federation. Why not *use* the Federation instead, with an eye to one day consuming it?

—*we're only moving them.*

(Taking their home, their privacy, their way of life . . .)

No. Simply moving them, so that the rest of the galaxy might live. Might be healed.

It was easy when Gallatin thought of them objectively, as a race; it was much harder when he remembered the specific individuals. When he remembered what it was like to think innocently, as they did, to wish no harm . . .

But they harmed you, Gallatin. Look at the diseased, decrepit thing you have become.

He stepped up behind Ru'afo, who was for the umpteenth time watching a simulation of the injection procedure. Over Ru'afo's shoulder, Gallatin watched the screen as the streamlined, elegantly small injector assembly sailed into the outermost of the planet's rings and fired bright blasts that flared blue, then surged through violet to red, flaring brighter, ever brighter, until at last the ring itself was consumed, trembling as if ablaze.

And then the next ring, and the next, until Gallatin beheld a world afire.

At his first viewing of it, he had thought it beautiful,

glorious; now it simply annoyed him, and made him anxious for it all to be done with. He judged Ru'afo's constant replaying of the simulation to be obsessive.

Ru'afo apparently sensed his second's presence, for he spoke first, without turning from the screen. "The injector performs perfectly in every situation. . . ."

"Sir," Gallatin said urgently, "as the *Enterprise* left orbit, one of their support craft went down to the surface."

Ru'afo swiveled in his chair at once, and took the padd Gallatin proffered him.

"It appeared to be the captain's yacht," Gallatin continued. "Five persons on board."

As he studied the padd, Ru'afo's expression grew stony—he was careful not to resplit the newly healed skin—then he looked up with eyes as hard, as determined, as Gallatin had ever seen. "We're not waiting until morning. Take the shuttles and get everyone off the surface tonight."

Gallatin nodded, and moved to turn—but paused as Ru'afo spoke again.

"Gallatin . . . if Picard or any of his people interfere . . . eliminate them."

It was the end of the world, Artim decided, even though the stories his father told him spoke only of a different world's demise. *This* world was supposed to go on forever. . . .

But as the boy stood in the dim, torchlit village square, watching Tournel ring the great summoning bell, he had never felt so afraid. Fear was in the night air: in the swift urgent movements of those who tied supplies onto the backs of pack animals, in the eyes of the children dragged along by their parents, in the voices of the adults—hundreds of them, the whole village—who cried out questions.

What is it?

What's going on?

What's happened?

Is something wrong?

There was even a faint undercurrent of terror in Tournel's shouted replies: *We're leaving the village . . . take only what you need . . . bring food . . . we may not be back for days. . . .*

Artim choked on the dust kicked up by the scurrying of so many people and animals, then started as a brilliant burst of light twinkled beside him. He swung about to see the artificial life-form, who had apparently just activated the device; the creature smiled slightly, comfortingly at him, and Artim wondered whether the smile was as artificial as its owner.

"It is a transport inhibitor," the life-form said. "It will help prevent Son'a ships from beaming anyone off the surface."

Overwhelmed by fright, Artim backed away, toward the group where his father—calm, solid, a fortress in the midst of all the chaos—stood talking with Anij and the starship captain.

At the moment, Picard was holding up the geoscans of the planet surface to Anij and Sojef. "These veins of kelbonite running through the hills will interfere with their transporters," he explained.

He paused as the boy Artim, wide-eyed as a frightened deer, stepped up and clung to his father. If Picard had harbored any doubts about the rightness of what he was doing, that single act erased them.

"When the terrain forces us away from the deposits," he continued, "we'll use transport inhibitors to compensate. The mountains have the highest concentrations of kelbonite; once we're there, transport will be virtually impossible."

"There are caves in those mountains," Anij said. Like Sojef, she had been listening keenly; but compared to his stolid calmness, she was a coil of energy waiting to spring, to take action.

Picard acknowledged her comment with a nod. "We can hold them off a long time . . . *once we get there.* . . . But they will not make it easy to get there."

He half turned, expectant, as Data and Worf approached.

"Captain," the android said. "We have activated transport inhibitors around the village."

"Good," Picard replied. "Let's move these people out."

Worf hesitated. "Should I distribute phasers to the Ba'ku, Sir?"

The captain shook his head. "No. We'll be responsible for that, Mister Worf."

There came a sudden roar overhead, in a sky that up to that instant had been silent; with the others, Picard looked up to see the lights of a Son'a shuttle-craft, bright, blinking, and malignant against the starlit dark.

Aboard that shuttlecraft, Gallatin studied the sensors, and came to the same conclusion just as his stunningly beautiful Elloran lieutenant stated, with a modicum of alarm: "Transporters are not functioning." Riva was her name—her only name, as the Ellora were not given to sur- or prenames, and she had a pale, exotic attractiveness and the wide hips much admired by the Son'a. Gallatin was expected to drool over her, and take sexual advantage of her as he wished; but in truth, he admired her professionalism, her intelligence, too much to do so. Ru'afo would be indignant if he found out, would say Gallatin was going soft—and perhaps he was.

But he treated her with as much respect as he could without the other Son'a noticing—the first time in his

life he had ever done so with one of his lieutenants—
and it seemed to him that she appreciated it, and
returned it. The Ellora always feigned devotion to
their masters; but all those who were able to betray
their masters in order to escape did.

Gallatin was not so certain that Riva would do the
same to him. At the very least, she would hesitate a
long moment. . . .

At the time, however, he ignored all thoughts of
Riva and her loyalty; right now, the sensors showed
something disturbing—something the damnably up-
right Picard was responsible for, no doubt.

"They're blocking the beams with some kind of
inhibitors," Gallatin said; his voice was calm, though
inwardly he cursed the starship captain. "We'll have
to locate and destroy them."

He had wanted it to go easily; wanted to do
whatever he could to avoid having to execute Ru'afo's
order concerning the Starfleet group. But Picard
seemed determined to make that impossible. . . .

Most of the villagers had made it through the open
fields into the meadow, with the uniformed Starfleet
people helping the village leaders to guide the crowd.
However, as they reached the narrow pass leading up
into the mountains, their progress slowed. By this
time, the exercise and his father Sojef's fearless de-

meanor had calmed Artim somewhat; he stood close beside Sojef at the mountain pass as his father called out—calmly, rationally as always—to the others:

"Don't try to carry too much. We've got a long climb ahead of us. . . ."

I'm safe, Artim reassured himself. *I'm safe, because my father's here, and he **always** knows the right thing to do. . . .*

Suddenly, the ground beneath him lurched, with such force that pebbles leapt into the air, slid down the pass; overhead, the sky boomed as if with mortally close thunder. Some of the people cried out; others dropped what they were carrying and began to move faster. Parents swept up children into their arms. Artim reached for his father's hand and caught it.

As long as Father's here, I can bear it. . . .

Another painful blast overhead; beside them, one of the brightly lit devices—a transport inhibitor, the artificial life-form had called it—exploded, then darkened. A brown-skinned Starfleet officer with a forehead that seemed made of wind-sculpted wood cried out to Captain Picard: "We've lost three transport inhibitors! There's a gap in the field. . . ."

Artim was not entirely certain what that meant, but he knew it boded ill. Sojef began to move, and Artim followed, trying hard to hold on to his father's hand in the moving wave of Ba'ku. They moved slowly at first, then faster, faster, pushed by those behind them, until they were running . . .

. . . running, beneath the roar of low-flying ships. Suddenly, to the front and the right, running Ba'ku shimmered and then *simply disappeared.* Artim at first doubted what he saw; but no, there was surprise too on Sojef's face, and a concern that made the boy feel a fresh thrill of fear. And it was not just one or two people who disappeared—no, it was a dozen, then twenty, thirty, *fifty.* . . .

A man in the crowd screamed; a child cried out a mother's name. Any semblance of civility was replaced by outright panic; the crowd began pushing harder now, harder, in its frenzy to reach the next transport inhibitor. With the peculiar helplessness one feels in the worst nightmares, Artim tried to hold on to his father's hand; tried, but felt himself slowly pushed away until he could touch nothing but his father's fingertips, even though Sojef struggled valiantly to maintain contact with his son. And then even fingertip-to-fingertip contact was broken, though Sojef's very gaze seemed enough, so determined it was to keep hold of the boy. Then even that was gone, as with horror Artim watched his father's form shimmer, then disappear as if it had never existed, had never set foot upon this path.

He stopped, as if waiting there might cause Sojef to

reappear in the same spot; but the crowd in its hysteria knocked him down. The colorful palm pet slipped from his pocket, out onto the ground, in enormous danger of being trampled. Through sheer will, Artim managed to recapture him, just as someone stepped hard on the crook of his upturned elbow. The boy cried out in pain and surprise as a new problem presented itself: He himself was in danger of being trampled. He glanced up to see a stream of ever-changing figures, dark and frantic against a night sky brightened by the lights of ships, by the shining transport inhibitors. Once, twice, three times Artim tried to push himself to his feet, but the Ba'ku were rushing like a flood, knocking him down, stepping on his feet and legs.

Artim lowered his head; terror and defeat overwhelmed him. Perhaps he should just accept his fate and die here, for he had no idea whether his father still lived.

And then a strong—a *very* strong—arm scooped him up, and held him against a warm chest as if he were still a small child. Artim looked up in total bewilderment at the pale golden face of the artificial life-form. His first instinct was to struggle, to break free of the alien grasp—but he was too tired, and also suddenly filled with an odd sense of trust. His own people had not stopped to help him; but this one had.

"My father . . ." he said plaintively.

"Your father has been transported to a spaceship," the life-form explained. "He has not been harmed."

Artim accepted the explanation utterly: for one thing, he was desperate to believe that Sojef was all right; for another, there was something so believable about the life-form that Artim could not doubt him.

He sighed, relaxed, and let himself be carried forward through the pushing crowd, past Captain Picard, who was calling out:

"Stay in the protected areas. We'll be safe when we get into the hills. . . ."

Inside the Son'a tactical room, the recently returned Gallatin pointed to the large wall display, a geoscan of the Ba'ku foothills. "They're following the kelbonite deposits," he told Ru'afo and Dougherty, "using the interference to block our transporters."

"Recommendations?" Ru'afo asked his two companions. A simple question, uttered in an even tone, but Dougherty sensed the fury lurking behind it, the accusation:

*If you had not been so meek, Starfleet admiral, if you had been firm and specific with the **Enterprise** captain from the beginning, if you had permitted my people to destroy that damned android—*

And why didn't I? Dougherty asked himself. During his long career, Matthew Dougherty had always been decisive, had always known what to do and when to do it. No one could ever have accused him of being mild-mannered or confused.

At least, not until Madalyn had died; it was as though, with her passing, she had taken something intangible from him: a certain strength, a certain confidence. He was weary now of conflict, of pain. He wanted only to ease them for himself and everyone else.

But at the moment, the admiral was filled with conflict—and anger. Anger at Ru'afo, for his damnable condescension; anger at Picard, for interfering; anger at himself, for being weak and indecisive, and for being embarrassed about it now, in front of the Son'a.

With all the harshness, all the firmness he could muster, Dougherty addressed the ahdar. "Take me down. Let me talk to Picard."

"Talk," Ru'afo sneered, with such infinite contempt that the admiral's cheeks went hot; had a Starfleet subordinate addressed him in that tone, court-martial would be imminent. As it was, Dougherty clenched his jaw, forced to swallow the insult. "We should send down an assault team."

The admiral straightened in his too-soft chair and in a low, dangerous voice began, "That is *not* an acceptable option. If people get hurt, all the support we have in the Federation—"

"Federation support, Federation procedures, Federation rules." Ru'afo drowned him out, dismissing all three concepts with the wave of a bejeweled hand. "Look in the mirror, Admiral. The Federation is *old.* In the last twenty-four months, it's been challenged by every major power in the quadrant: the Borg, the Cardassians, the Dominion. . . . They all smell the scent of death on the Federation. That's why you've embraced our offer—because it will give your dear Federation new life. Well, how badly do you want it, Admiral? Because there are hard choices to be made now."

He paused, giving Dougherty a breath's space to respond; but Dougherty was too busy thinking about how badly *he,* personally, wanted youth, health, a few extra centuries of life; a few extra centuries avoiding the pain Madalyn had felt, of losing everyone, everything, that was important to her.

Ru'afo continued, relentless. "If the *Enterprise* gets through with news about their brave captain's valiant struggle on behalf of the defenseless Ba'ku, your Federation politicians will waver, your Federation opinion polls will open a public debate, your Federation allies will want their say. . . . Need I go on?"

Dougherty drew in a deep breath and broke off eye contact. There *was* nothing further to say; his choice was clear. Certainly, a greatly extended lifespan—virtual immortality—and perfect health were worth the relocation of six hundred people.

Were they worth the killing of Picard and his crew?

It was Gallatin, the subahdar—kinder, more reasonable Gallatin, always reluctant to choose violence—who offered up an option. "There is an alternative to an all-out assault," he told Ru'afo, while Dougherty studied his palms. "Isolinear tags would allow our transporters to lock onto them."

Ru'afo dismissed it at once—as the admiral knew he would. "We'd have to tag every one of them. That would take time—and we don't have it. The *Enterprise* is only nineteen hours from communications range with the Federation—"

Dougherty looked up at once. "I'll order Riker to turn around."

Smirking, Ru'afo eyed him. "Picard's first officer. Do you really believe he'll listen?"

And with that small question, whatever shred of confidence Dougherty had left disintegrated, and he looked on Ru'afo with undisguised hatred. Ru'afo noted it, his smirk widening faintly.

"My ships are capable of intercepting the *Enterprise* before it reaches the perimeter," the Son'a said. "I could send them to . . . escort . . . it back. But Commander Riker might not want to come."

There it was, the choice: the lives of a thousand or more people versus the rest of the galaxy.

For an instant, no more, Dougherty closed his eyes and thought of Madalyn, and that terrible last day.

And then he opened his eyes, and with a pain that felt like a coiled serpent squeezing tight around his gut, said:

"Send your ships. . . ."

Dawn was turning the sky rosy against the mountains as the Ba'ku, now deep into the foothills, wound their way into the steeper terrain near the mountains. The people were calmer now, perhaps because they knew they were safer here, or perhaps because they were simply exhausted from the long trek.

As for Artim, exhaustion had taken the edge off his sorrow and worry: he believed the artificial life-form—which the others called Data—when it said Sojef was safe. At the same time, the boy could not help worrying about what *might* happen to his father. What if he never saw him again?

The thought, combined with Artim's physical tiredness, brought him to the edge of tears; to fight it off, he distracted himself by glancing over at the life-form—at Data. Clearly, Data was artificial—he showed no sign whatsoever of weariness, despite the hours of walking.

At the same time, he had been very protective of Artim, and had not left him since Sojef had disappeared. He hadn't let go of the boy until he was sure it was safe to do so, and then from time to time he had put a reassuring hand on the boy's shoulder when

Artim was close to weeping. It was becoming very hard for Artim to think of Data as simply a machine.

Cautiously, the boy glanced sidewise at the android and said, "My father told me I shouldn't talk to you."

Pale golden face perfectly composed, Data glanced down at the boy. "I understand." His expression was one of real, living life-form compassion; at the same time, he did not breathe, did not gasp with exertion as did the others around them as they climbed the hills, and there was a quirkiness to the movements of his face and hands that seemed unnatural—as if he were trying too hard to copy human gestures and couldn't quite pull them off.

"I don't," Artim admitted honestly.

Data frowned slightly at that, and cocked his head like a curious bird.

The boy sighed, uncomfortable at saying anything that might seem disloyal to his father. "Not everyone here agrees with him," he confessed in a low voice. "I mean, you know, about machines. There was even a big fight about it once." He paused, then studied Data's face frankly. "Do you *like* being a machine?"

Data looked away, considering the question thoughtfully. The act pleased Artim; Sojef always answered his son's questions thoughtfully, and never laughed at them, the way some of the adults did. At last the android replied, "I aspire to be more than I am."

"I know why," the boy said swiftly. Data gave him the curious-bird look again, as if to say, *How did you guess?* "So people like us won't be afraid of you anymore."

The answer seemed to surprise the android; but once again, he considered it thoroughly, then allowed, "Perhaps."

The trail grew abruptly steep; Artim groaned as his thigh muscles burned with effort. He remained speechless, gasping, until the slope eased; then he turned again to the android, who was carefully matching his pace to the child's.

"Don't you ever get tired?" Artim asked, with just a hint of irritation.

Data shook his head. "My power cells continually recharge themselves."

"I can't imagine what it would be like to be a machine."

Data studied the boy for a long time. "Perhaps it would surprise you to know that *I* have often tried to imagine what it would be like to be a child."

"Really?" For some reason, Artim found this surprising.

"Really." Data's amber eyes focused steadily on Artim, and the boy realized that the android wanted to learn from him.

The path grew steep once more, and Artim sighed with effort; once again, he noticed that the android compensated by taking smaller steps. "For one thing," Artim gasped, "your legs are shorter than everyone else's."

"But they are in a constant state of growth," Data countered. "Do you find it difficult to adapt?"

"Adapt?" Artim frowned at him, puzzled.

He tried again: "A child's specifications are never the same from one moment to the next. It is a wonder you do not trip over your own feet."

Artim blinked at him, suddenly understanding his own clumsiness. "Sometimes I do."

Data nodded, frowning slightly as if making mental notes. "My legs are eighty-seven-point-two centimeters. They were eighty-seven-point-two centimeters the day I was created. They will be eighty-seven-point-two centimeters the day I go off-line. My operation depends on specifications that do not change." He paused to look down at his lower limbs. "I will never know the experience of growing up . . . or tripping over my own feet."

Artim absorbed this, intrigued, his own weariness temporarily forgotten. "But you've never had adults telling you what to do all the time . . . or bedtimes . . . or having to eat food you don't like. . . ."

"I would gladly accept the requirement of a bedtime in exchange for knowing what it is like to be a child," Data said simply.

There was a wistfulness in his tone that made Artim

want to help, to do whatever he could to help this kind . . . life-form. He thought a moment, then asked, "Do machines ever play?"

"I play the violin," Data said, "and my chess routines are quite advanced. . . ."

"No." Artim shook his head. "I mean, haven't you ever just played for *fun?*"

Data drew back his head slightly, tucking in his chin. "Androids don't have . . . *fun.*"

With an air of authority, Artim told him: "Look, if you want to know what it's like to be a child, you need to learn to play."

Data digested this quietly; the two of them fell silent and continued, along with the others, the ascent into the mountains and the day.

A tired but exuberant Picard made his way along the trail, amazed by his own endurance, by Anij's. She had remained beside him for the entire hike. Though they had remained silent most of the way, their breath had fallen into the same rhythm, as had their pace, and it seemed to Picard that they were no longer two separate entities, but one. . . .

A few hours ago, they had entered a part of the trail flanked on either side by towering peaks, so beautifully carved by wind and sand Picard was reminded of his homeland's great Gothic cathedrals. Now dawn was peering through the latticework, over the tops of stones, turning the rock from black to aubergine to purple-brown. Behind them, a long line of Ba'ku with occasional pack animals trailed, in a scene reminiscent of the biblical exodus . . . though, Picard remarked to himself grimly, that one had not taken place in Paradise.

The scattering of pebbles behind him, the thud of someone scrambling up the trail; Picard turned to see Worf hurrying toward him. The Klingon had definitely lost a wrinkle or two in his time on the Ba'ku planet, and his hair seemed to have grown thicker, wilder, giving him a leonine look.

The captain paused in his trek to allow Worf to catch up to him; once the Klingon was alongside him, Picard smiled faintly. "Mister Worf, you need a haircut."

Worf glanced downward, clearly embarrassed. "Accelerated hair growth is often experienced by Klingons during *Jak'tahla.*"

Anij took a step closer to Picard. *"Jak'tahla?"*

Under his voice, Picard explained: "Roughly translated: puberty. Although for a Klingon that's not doing it justice. . . ." Aloud to Worf, he said, "Any severe mood swings, unusual aggressive tendencies, be sure to let me know right away."

"Yes, Captain," the Klingon replied, eyes downcast with embarrassment; at last, he revealed the reason he had come. "The Ba'ku could use some rest, sir.

According to the geoscan, this may be the safest area for the next few kilometers."

"Very well," Picard said. "We'll take an hour. Break out some rations."

Worf nodded again, then gave a reverberating shout and waved his arm in the air. Gradually, the moving column of people stopped, and sat down along the trail. The Klingon returned to his position lower on the trail, while Picard, with Anij at his side, moved forward through blooming sage-scented brush in order to better see the path ahead. On the banks of a running brook, not far from a mountain waterfall that sent cool shimmering droplets into the air, the captain stopped to rest.

The two of them sat cross-legged, his left knee pressed against her right; as aware as he was of her touch, he pulled from his belt a pair of field glasses and examined in more detail what faced them. More brush, then another ridge, this one not so steep. . . .

Anij pointed with a graceful arm. "Right beyond that ridge is where the caves begin. We can hide for days."

He did not share her enthusiasm; he remembered the fury in Ru'afo's eyes. The ahdar was not going to let this be easy. "By now the Son'a have scanned the area and know that just as well as we do."

She had no answer for that, but did not seem to

share his seriousness as he lifted the glasses back to his eyes and surveyed the territory still to be crossed. The openness of it disturbed him, as did its distance from the main veins of kelbonite. It *should* be safe, but if it wasn't . . .

He jumped and pulled the glasses down, startled by a soft, tickling stroke across the bare crown of his head.

Anij was smiling, her gaze frankly seductive. "It's been three hundred years since I've seen a bald man."

He grinned back at her, surprised . . . and delighted. With sudden boldness, he asked, "How is it a woman like you never married? And don't tell me you 'just haven't gotten around to it yet. . . .' "

She blinked her eyes, coyly innocent. "What's the rush?" And she swiveled about so that they sat face-to-face.

So, his feelings for her were returned; the knowledge brought with it a thrill of exhilaration. Huskily, Picard said, "I should warn you. . . . I've always been attracted to older women. . . ."

In reply, she took his hands in hers.

At that instant, Picard's world slowed: until that moment he had not noticed the delicate breeze upon his skin; now he felt it, heard it sigh in his ears as it lowered in pitch. Sight took on an intensity near-anguishing in its beauty: the droplets spawned by the

waterfall took on prismatic brilliance, each hovering
in the air like a miniature gem; the cascade of water
itself took on the indistinct texture of velvet.

Following Anij's lead, Picard knelt beside the water, watched as, with one hand, she plucked a single
cobalt bloom from the bank and blew the petals into
the air; she smiled with childlike glee as the petals
slowly, slowly ascended into the shimmering air,
hovered seconds, then just as slowly descended to
earth.

"How are you doing this?" Picard breathed, fascinated.

She smiled. "No more questions."

She turned her gaze from him, and he followed it
across the brook to the other bank, where a humming-
bird drank from a crimson flower, the beat of its
wings languid, lazy.

Then she guided his hand in hers into the brook
beside them, and he felt the cool water flow through
his fingers, embrace every atom of flesh, bone, and
muscle with tactile pleasure, with sheer aliveness
almost too pleasurable to bear.

And when he thought he could bear it no longer,
Anij drew their hands from the water, skin glistening.
With her other hand, she touched his arm—and now
it was not just the world, but Anij and Picard themselves who slowed. . . .

He heard his own heart beating slowly, heard the

gentle thrum of blood in his veins, and the sigh of his own breath, uneven with excitement. Anij blinked, and he heard the whisper of her lashes, the drum of her eyelids as they came together, then opened over those starlit eyes—eyes that were bright, then brighter, as if aglow with a growing life force . . . and he knew at once why he loved her, just as he loved the stars: because she was radiant, mysterious, ancient.

Her fingers brushed gently against the hair at the top of his chest. Each hair felt alive, separate, reacting with pure sensual enjoyment to even the lightest touch. . . . Picard half closed his eyes at the rapture of touch, even of sound, of her fingertips against his flesh.

And then she leaned forward, and brushed her lips—soft, delicate, full—against his. Gently, her teeth nipped his lower lip, and tugged it lightly, teasingly. . . .

At last her lips found his, and pressed full against them for eternity, as Picard surrendered himself to bliss. . . .

NINE

☆

Aboard the *Enterprise,* Will Riker sat at command and checked the viewscreen for the thousandth time: nothing, save spectacular white and rose-gold displays of gaseous debris. At one-third impulse, the *Enterprise* was still wading slowly—*too* slowly, Riker decided—through the Briar Patch. A sixth sense, one developed after years of starship duty, had set off a silent alarm in his head. Something was about to happen, something not good.

Perhaps, Riker reasoned with himself, at least part of his apprehension came from his rekindled passion for Deanna; it had been enormously difficult to leave her on the planet surface, at the mercy of the Son'a. He missed her presence on the bridge, though it was now in the hands of Perim, La Forge, Daniels . . . and himself. He had a great deal to lose now, and if she were injured or, God forbid, killed before the *Enterprise* managed to reach the outskirts of the Patch—

Knock it off, he told himself, and mentally as well as physically straightened in his chair. *You're on duty, Mister.* . . . The reminder worked, just as it had during the first affair with Deanna, so long ago; Riker set his brain back to work on strategy for the inevitable.

Admiral Dougherty would not, of course, permit the Son'a to pursue the *Enterprise*—or at least, Riker could not conceive of such a thing. However, Riker didn't trust the Son'a; they could still come after the *Enterprise.*

And if they did . . . Well, they had faster ships and stronger weapons. The outcome would be inevitable. . . .

Would be, except that Riker had come up with a plan of his own to deal with them—Plan A, which might very well backfire, so he was searching for a Plan B. . . .

He was lost in thought a few minutes before—inevitably—the Trill, Perim, swiveled her head so that a singular cord stood out on her delicate neck, with its neat rows of irregular taupe markings against beige flesh. "Commander," she said, with the ancient calm associated with her race, "I'm showing two Son'a ships on an intercept course."

"How long till they reach us?" Riker asked.

"Eighteen minutes."

From ops, Geordi La Forge said, "We're not going to be able to get a transmission out of here for at least another hour. . . ."

Daniels spoke up from tactical. "They're hailing us."

Time for the first part of Plan A. Stroking an absent beard, Riker ordered: "Tell them our transceiver assembly is down, that we can send messages but can't receive them."

Daniels complied, hands moving swiftly over his companel. A long moment passed on the bridge before the lieutenant looked up and said, "I don't think they believe us."

Riker looked askance. "Why not?"

The answer came in the muted boom of an explosion well off-target; the ship shuddered gently. Riker glanced down immediately at his monitor for a sensor reading and curled his lip at the predictable result. "A photon torpedo." His tone went wry. "Isn't that the universal greeting when communications are down?"

La Forge countered quickly, "I think it's the universal greeting when you don't like someone."

Another off-target explosion rocked the ship gently.

"Full impulse," Riker demanded.

Just as he expected, La Forge took issue. "The

manifolds can't handle full impulse in the Patch, Commander. . . ."

It was true, of course; even so, Riker silenced the engineer with a look. "If we don't outrun them, the manifolds are going to be the only thing left of this ship."

La Forge drew in a breath, then nodded obediently. "I'll be in engineering."

As Geordi left—his post quickly replaced by another officer—Riker called out: "Red alert! All hands, battle stations!"

Picard, his heart open with joy, was walking hand-in-hand with Anij back toward the others—specifically, toward Worf and Data—when he saw the Son'a come.

Twelve shuttles in formation, shining and sinister in the morning light; at once, his joy dimmed, then transformed into fear, anger, and determination all at once. The vessels neatly, evenly, divided the airspace above the Ba'ku encampment, then hovered a moment—a terrible one. Picard felt a cold thrill descend on him despite the sun's growing warmth, and thought: *Ru'afo has had his way, and they have come to kill us.*

But no, the vessels never fired; they were pregnant with a different evil. As Picard and the others watched in horror, each shuttle gave birth to a dozen or more drones—silver, whirring, twice the size of a large human's fist.

And *alive*—blinking red, blue, white, scanning, sensing. . . . Then, like furious hornets, they descended from the sky in swarms and assailed their targets.

The Ba'ku scattered. Picard instinctively grabbed his phaser and began firing, as did Worf nearby—and Data, who stood protectively in front while his young charge, Artim, retired intelligently behind the nearest boulder.

The captain managed to destroy one drone, the Klingon another, but a third drone in the swarm managed to launch a small, nonplasma weapon. Swiftly, it struck its mark—the back of a Ba'ku woman, just beneath her left shoulder—and before Picard or anyone else could react, she dematerialized in front of them. The captain fired on the drone; it dissolved with a small burst of flame and a sizzle—too late, too late. Around the Starfleet officers, Ba'ku were scattering, and dematerializing. . . .

"Isolinear tags," Worf shouted, telling the captain what he had already figured out for himself. "Their transporters can lock onto them."

"We have to find shelter," Picard countered, but he was looking to Anij for the answer.

She pointed with admirable self-possession, if not calm. "There's a cavern at the base of the next hill. . . ."

Picard made a large, sweeping gesture to the entire encampment. "This way!"

The Ba'ku began to move, as close to a run as possible, given the number of people. The captain and his officers continued firing—but the odds were against them; for every drone they managed to destroy, two or three more arrived to take its place.

It was going to be difficult to hold on, Picard knew; and he wondered whether the *Enterprise* had made it out of the Patch. . . .

At the moment, the *Enterprise* bridge was a study in battle damage: cracked conduits leaked plasma, smoke streamed from a few off-line consoles. The ship was still exchanging fire with the two pursuing Son'a ships, though in the Briar Patch, the weapons were as likely to miss as hit their targets. The crew, too, were looking a bit worse for wear, their faces and uniforms smudged with soot.

As for Riker, he was on his feet, Son'a plasma weapons be damned. The instant engineering took the *Enterprise* up to full impulse, he could hear the engines straining; Geordi had been right about the ship not being able to handle the speed, but Riker had gambled on the Son'a intercepting them a little later. . . . Apparently, full impulse was not a huge difficulty for them.

Time to start thinking again about Plan B.

"Shields at sixty percent!" Daniels announced.

Almost simultaneously, La Forge's plaintive voice filtered over the com. "Engineering to bridge. We're burning deuterium down here." Riker heard hissing in the background: no doubt the sound of engineers spraying coolant on the engines to keep temperatures from redlining. "We're going to blow *ourselves* up," La Forge continued. "We won't need any help from the Son'a."

Riker listened, then ended the communication without comment; he was distracted by the sight on the forward viewscreen. He took a step forward to stand directly behind Ensign Perim's chair at conn. "What's inside that nebula cluster?" He gestured with his chin at the screen.

Perim checked her sensors. "Cometary debris, pockets of unstable metreon gas. . . . We don't want to go in there, Sir."

"Yes, we do." Riker ignored her sharp glance up at him. "I'll take it from here, Ensign."

She rose and moved over to ops; Riker slid behind the conn and smiled grimly to himself. "Time to use the Briar Patch like Br'er Rabbit did. . . ."

Picard stood close enough now to the mouth of the cavern to feel the steam and smell the sulfur of the hot mineral springs hidden inside, but he never took his eyes off the sky and the swarms of drones that kept coming. More and more Ba'ku were dematerializing despite his firing his phaser until his fingertip was numb on the trigger, despite his shouting again and again, until his throat was hoarse: "Into the cavern! Move!"

Beside him, Worf roared as his phaser malfunctioned; Picard watched with peripheral vision as the howling Klingon swung his rifle like a *bat'leth* at a drone. His first attempt missed, but a second drone, then a third, were not so lucky; Worf struck them full on with the rifle butt, disabling them and sending them flying what Picard imagined was a full kilometer.

Afterward, the Klingon glanced at his captain and growled, "Definitely feeling aggressive tendencies . . ."

Once again, Artim saw how technology could be used to do horrible, hurtful things; at the same time, he felt safest running next to the artificial life-form Data, who kept firing what he called a phaser in order to destroy the miniature silver ships. In fact, as the two ran together, surrounded by a cluster of Ba'ku, Data did his best to shield Artim with his body from the terrible little ships. That morning, Artim had thought he could walk no farther—but the terror generated in him by the attack fueled him so that he ran full speed up a very steep trail alongside a sheer cliff.

Suddenly, one of the bad people—a Son'a, accompanied by two soldiers of a different race—appeared in front of them all on the treacherous ledge. They had come to take prisoners, Artim realized, and cried out in fear; at the same time, he looked to Data, wondering: would the android fire his phaser and disintegrate them, just as he had the little ships?

Would he kill? Father would rather die himself. . . .

Artim barely finished the thought when Data ran, lunging low and spreading his arms, into the three males—knocking them cleanly off the cliff. It was a long, fatal fall to the bottom, Artim knew, and the boy released a silent sob. He had trusted Data to be different from what he had heard of offlanders; he had credited him with morals and a heart, but now . . .

Father was right. *All* technology was wicked. The artificial life-form could not be trusted, after all.

Yet even as Artim wept inwardly, the android snatched one of the little ships clean from the air, and aimed it at the three falling men. The device whirred, then shot an almost invisible blur toward the three: tiny metallic objects, Artim knew, that looked like a piece of jewelry. They must have hit their falling targets, because one instant, the three men were there—then the next, they were gone. *Dematerialized,* Data called it, which meant they were now safe back aboard their own ship.

Despite his fear, Artim grinned, faith restored,

while Data crushed the device in his hands. Almost instantly, he returned to Artim's side, and began firing again at the little ships overhead.

The ride aboard the *Enterprise* was rough, so rough that Riker fancied he felt his internal organs vibrating; so rough that when Lieutenant Daniels spoke, it was in vibrato:

"Sir, they've detonated an isolytic burst. A subspace tear is forming."

"On screen," Riker ordered.

The scene on the main viewer shifted to show an actual rift in space—a jagged, growing no-thingness that was darker than black; certainly, darker than the glowing Briar Patch. In an instant, it would consume the *Enterprise* and spit her out into normal space, where she would be a sitting duck for the fast Son'a ships.

From ops, Perim murmured, "I thought subspace weapons were banned by the Khitomer Accords. . . ."

"Remind me to lodge a protest," Riker said. It came out a little more sarcastically than he'd meant it to—he didn't want Perim to think he was implying she was an idiot to state the obvious—but at the moment, he was too busy thinking of ways to save the ship to worry about her feelings. He was on the verge of contacting engineering when La Forge's voice came over com.

"Commander, our warp core is acting like a magnet to the tear. We're pulling it like a zipper across space."

"Options?" Riker demanded.

On the other side of the link, La Forge drew a long breath. Then: "We could eject the core."

"Will that stop the tear?" Riker didn't miss even a beat; there wasn't time. On the viewscreen, the tear kept moving closer. . . .

"You got me, Commander."

Riker drew up, scowling; that was *not* the answer he wanted. "That's your expert opinion?"

"Detonating the warp core *might* neutralize the cascade," Geordi explained swiftly. "But then again, it might not. Subspace weapons are unpredictable. That's why they were banned."

"The tear is closing on us," Daniels called. "Impact in fifteen seconds."

"Eject the core," Riker told La Forge.

"I just did."

"Impact in ten seconds," Daniels counted down.

"Detonate!" Riker ordered.

And he drew in a breath as the blacker-than-blackness came looming toward them, as if space itself were a delicate centuries-old piece of cloth being ripped down the middle, with the *Enterprise* at dead center. . . .

Abruptly, the darkness dissolved in an all-consuming flash of whiter-than-white, one that blinded Riker even through his instinct-closed eyelids. This, he knew, was the warp core exploding, with such magnitude that, for an instant, the entire universe, Riker himself included, seemed made of pure light.

Then the first wave hit, and threw him down hard. His chin struck the console with dazing force; disoriented, still blinded by the afterimage, Riker was slammed to the deck. He fell hard on his right shoulder, sending a jolt of pain down his spine, his arm.

He gritted his teeth, waiting: either the *Enterprise* would now be destroyed, or the spatial disturbance would ease, permitting him to get back on his feet and assess the damage to the ship.

And there *was* damage to her: he could hear the thud of panels being blown off bulkheads, of other bodies falling around him; could smell fire and smoke. As his vision gradually cleared, he could see the bridge lights flicker, then dim.

Slowly, slowly, the ship righted herself. As quickly as he could—which wasn't very—Riker crawled back to conn.

As he pulled himself up into his chair, Daniels— who was first to make it back to his station—called out, excited: "It worked, Commander! The tear's been sealed!"

Immediately, La Forge's voice filtered over com

(and Riker permitted himself a small, inward smile of relief to know Geordi had made it through the particularly rough ride). The engineer's tone was somber, warning. "There's nothing to stop them from doing it again—and we're fresh out of warp cores."

Ensign Perim—her delicate features smudged, her long, formerly bound hair hanging half loose onto her shoulders—turned toward Riker. *If **she** looks that bad, then what the devil do **I** look like?* the commander wondered, as he listened to her deliver the final blow. "We're still thirty-six minutes from transmission range, sir."

Riker nodded, releasing a heavy sigh as he instinctively clutched his right upper arm, to prevent further stabs of pain. Plan A had failed; Plan B had worked, but was only a temporary fix. He was forced to go to Plan C—reluctantly, because it was the riskiest plan of all.

Aloud, he announced: "We're through running from these bastards. . . ."

With Worf and Anij resting by his side, Picard stood near the mouth of the hydrothermal cavern and stared at the small silver drones hovering menacingly on the other side of a force field. Occasionally, one of the drones would bump the field, causing it to spark and hum . . . but for the most part, the drones simply waited.

And time might just be on their side; Picard was beginning to nurse serious doubts about the *Enterprise*'s safety. If Ru'afo—with or without Dougherty's consent—was this desperate to get his hands on the Ba'ku . . .

The cave's interior was humid as a sauna, thanks to an underground hot spring; briny, sulfurous water pooled on the ground, requiring the Ba'ku and their pack animals to slosh through mud before finding a dry spot to settle in. Worf's dark face had taken on a glistening sheen; Anij's paler one was flushed and shining. Picard wiped his forehead with the inside of his wrist and drew away sweat.

He turned from the cavern's mouth to regard the scene behind him. The cavern's entrance, where he, Anij, and Worf sat, was dry—but the path immediately descended and was filled ankle-deep with thin, pale mud, a mixture of water and the limestone-based rock that formed the cavern walls. The Ba'ku had had to wade through several meters of this until they made it to dry ground, and the largest "room," where most of them, including Data's little friend, Artim, sat exhausted alongside their pack animals. The rest had wandered farther back into the cavern along narrow "corridors" and settled on other suitably dry places.

From one of these corridors, Data emerged, and walked without a trace of gingerness through the slippery mud toward his captain.

"How many?" Picard asked darkly, when the android had arrived.

"Another forty-three people reported taken, sir."

The captain frowned, sighing—but the sound was immediately interrupted by loud booms overhead; beneath his feet, the earth shuddered.

Fearful murmurs came from the nearest Ba'ku encampment. One of the pack animals bleated and tried to run; its owner rose at once and tried to calm it. Data turned to visually locate Artim, with a paternal concern that was touching; the boy was clearly frightened, as was his little "palm pet," which had crawled out of his pocket onto his arm.

Another blast came—then another, and another, until the ground beneath shook continuously, and sand—damp though it was—began to drop from the cavern's ceiling.

The captain exchanged a grim look with Worf.

"They're trying to force us out so their drones can tag us," the Klingon said, staring outward and upward from the cavern entrance. Picard nodded. Given the amount of sand starting to rain down, it seemed Ru'afo just might get his way. . . .

Data, meantime, was calmly studying a readout on his tricorder. "With all the hydrothermal vents in the substrata, the structural integrity is not going to hold for long, Captain."

Picard stared back at the mouth of the cavern, and

the half dozen drones hovering behind the force field. Waiting . . .

Hands spread, beseeching, he turned toward Anij. "Is there any other way out of here?"

Grimly, she shook her head.

"Tracking the water's course may reveal another exit," Data suggested.

Picard made a "please do" gesture, then followed the android as Data began scanning the pale walls with the tricorder.

The two of them moved deeper into the cavern, deeper, until they passed all of the frightened Ba'ku and skittish animals. The passageway gradually narrowed, until they were forced to proceed single file through pungent, slippery mud, with Data and his tricorder leading.

At last, Data stopped—at a place where the water had become a trickle and disappeared beneath a gray-white wall of stone.

During all this time, the overhead booms continued; the ground—as well as the android's voice—vibrated as he aimed the tricorder at the wall and reported: "I'm showing a nitrogen-oxygen flow behind this calcite formation, Captain."

Picard considered this. "Will the structure hold if we blast through?"

Data aimed the tricorder at the supporting walls, then looked up. "I believe it is safe, sir."

The captain drew his phaser; Data followed suit, and together they burned a hole into the limestone wall.

Picard stepped through first into a lighter, airier cave with a large natural exit. What he saw beyond it made him smile faintly; several different paths led up to the nearby mountains, where a half dozen cave openings could be seen.

"Spread out as far as you can," Picard ordered, his gaze still on the goal. "Get everyone into those caves, set up force fields once you're inside. . . ."

Data nodded, and the two of them hurried back, sloshing water as they ran, to gather up the Ba'ku.

Aboard a barely functional bridge, Will Riker sat at conn, staring hard at the main viewscreen. On it, irregularly shaped gas pockets adorned the cosmic debris with glints of red, green, gold shot through with starlight.

By now, Riker's shoulder and back were causing him real anguish—but rather than dim his determination, the pain only served to fuel it. He'd be damned if he'd let the Son'a win now; damned if he'd let the *Enterprise* be destroyed, and leave the away team, especially Deanna, at the mercy of those criminals.

"Geordi," Riker demanded of the comlink, "are those pockets of metreon gas?"

From engineering, La Forge answered—sounding as bedraggled as Riker felt. "Aye, sir. Highly volatile. I recommend we keep our distance."

"Negative," Riker said. "I want to use the ram-scoop to collect as much of it as we can." The instant he said it, he became aware that every eye on the bridge was focused on him; and he heard, on the other side of the comlink, Geordi's slow intake of breath.

"The purpose being . . . ?" La Forge asked, with a tone that hinted the explanation was going to have to be *exceptionally* good to get the chief engineer's approval.

"The purpose being I intend to shove it down the Son'a's throat," Riker told him, with an intensity that said, **This** *is what I'm going to do, Mister, and the hell with what the rest of you think.*

"Commander." Daniels spoke up, clearly dismayed. "If one of their weapons hits that gas—"

Riker turned to Daniels with eyes so steely the lieutenant fell silent at once. "It's our only way out of here, Mister Daniels."

Down in engineering, Geordi La Forge cursed silently as another drop of sweat slid from his forehead into his eyes; he used the edge of his index finger to wipe his brow, then wiped the dripping finger against the side of his uniform. Before she left, Doctor Crusher had coached him on the use of his natural eyes, but she had never mentioned the fact that sweat—and a surprising number of other things, including smoke—would make his eyes sting.

And engineering was *hot*, still hot after the ejection of the warp core, and still filled with a steamy haze from the coolant sprayed on the engine. Not only had Doctor Crusher not mentioned the business about sweat stinging, she'd never said anything about steam or gas interfering with his vision. During the battle, La Forge's efficiency had been seriously hampered by his natural—and curtailed—eyesight.

But despite his frustration—and his fear of what the Son'a might do next—La Forge nodded with pure admiration at Riker's words, even as he, Geordi, moved to the nearest engineering console and worked feverishly to deploy the ramscoop.

It's our only way out of here, Mister Daniels.

As he manipulated the controls and squinted at the readout that showed the scoop gathering up gas pockets, Geordi said to com: "I wouldn't be surprised if history remembers this as the Riker maneuver."

"If it works," the commander countered, with typical Rikerian drollness.

La Forge grinned. "Even if it doesn't, they'll be teaching kids at the academy *not* to do this for years to come." Another drop of sweat stung his eye; again, he swore silently as he blinked, trying to force his vision to clear. It was an annoyingly slow process, gathering up information from all the different readouts via natural eyesight—and time was one thing they didn't have.

Without lifting his gaze from the console, La Forge complained aloud to the nearest ensign: "How do you people get anything done with such limited eyes? I'm ready to get my implants back." Sensors indicated that the ramscoop had reached its limits; the engineer hit his combadge. "Bridge."

On the bridge, Riker listened as Geordi's voice filtered over com. "Storage cells are at maximum capacity," La Forge reported. "Five thousand cubic meters of metreon gas."

Riker wasted no time acknowledging. Salvation— or death—would occur in a matter of seconds now. "Computer—access manual steering column."

In less than a heartbeat, the sleek column popped up from the console. "Transfer helm controls to manual," Riker ordered, grabbing the device, which fit comfortably in his palm.

In reply, the computer bleeped. The screen display shifted to reveal the two Son'a vessels—looming ever larger as the *Enterprise* closed in on them.

"They're powering their forward weapons array," Perim reported tersely.

"Blow out the ramscoop," Riker said, staring intently at the hostile ships. If death was coming, it would arrive in the next heartbeat or two—and he wanted to see it coming. He programmed the main screen to keep the Son'a in sight, despite the upcoming maneuver.

"Ramscoop released!" La Forge called from engineering.

Riker pressed a control on the column. At once, the *Enterprise* lurched, swinging away in a 180-degree arc—at the irritatingly slow pace of one-third impulse. *Move,* he urged the ship silently. ***Move . . .***

If she failed now to put enough space between herself and her attackers, she, too, would be destroyed.

On screen, a brilliant blast of plasma emerged from each of the Son'a vessels—only to be caught in the large translucent globe of gas directly in front of them. For a breathtakingly beautiful instant, the globe flared, radiant as a star gone nova . . . then exploded in a fiery burst.

Once again, Riker was slammed against the console—by momentum, as the force of the explosion sent the *Enterprise* hurtling away at full impulse. With enormous effort, the commander managed to raise his face and arms enough to grasp the manual control.

At the same time, he caught a glimpse of the receding Son'a ships—one disintegrating into fiery debris, the other intact but ablaze. For an instant, a faint, grim smile played on his lips. . . .

Until, that is, the manual control proved unresponsive. Riker fought desperately to regain control of the helm, but the ship was careening out of control. . . .

TEN

Ground and sky still thundered as Picard and his officers led another group of some seventy Ba'ku through the hole drilled in the pale calcite wall, then out through the new exit where several paths led toward other nearby caves. They had already herded several groups to safety; only one—which included Anij—remained in the original cavern. She had refused to leave with the first groups, insisting that her unofficial status as one of the secondary town leaders required her to help Tournel keep those remaining behind calm, and to ready them when the time came to leave.

Picard did not argue, could do nothing but respect her decision, admire her bravery. And while he left a good deal of his heart behind with her, he as always took his entire mind and attention with him when he helped the Ba'ku cross the short but unsheltered path from old cavern to new.

With Worf nearby, Picard ran at the head of the group of Ba'ku. Most of the group was coughing: the explosions had contaminated the sweet air with dust that slightly obscured vision and stung the back of the throat. The evacuation process was ungainly at best, with the pack animals now squealing, surly, and sometimes bolting (and, Picard noted, none too sweet-smelling), small children stumbling, and over-burdened adults occasionally dropping supplies in the path and stopping abruptly to pick them up. Most of all, the captain pitied Crusher, who was in the center of the group, and Data and Troi, who were bringing up the rear—all of them following where the animals had already trodden. But the Ba'ku men and women were strong and surefooted, despite their exhaustion, over the steep, uneven terrain.

The group was not far from the targeted cave when Picard's peripheral vision was seared by spontaneous brilliance—once, twice. Again. Beside him, Worf halted abruptly and pointed. "Up there!"

Behind the crest of a nearby ridge, a small squadron of Elloran and Tarlac soldiers squatted, along with their more elaborately dressed Son'a commander.

Picard blinked to dull the afterimages; at the same

time, new blasts of plasma came perilously close to the weary evacuees. "Data, Troi," the captain called, through his temporary blindness. "Keep these people moving. Worf, with me . . ."

At once, the android and Troi raced to the front of the crowd and began leading their charges away from the attack, toward the mountains. Picard detached his phaser from his belt while Worf took an ominously large weapon—a double-barreled isomagnetic disintegrator—from his backpack.

The captain fired—once, twice, three times— wounding one of the Tarlac and eating away at the ridge overhead, until Worf at last hoisted the huge disintegrator in his arms and took aim.

The blast provoked searing pain in Picard's ears, rattled his teeth; half deafened, he watched as part of the crest vibrated, then spilled down the hill as individual grains of sand. The force of the explosion hurled the soldiers backward—all except the Son'a officer, who fell forward and rolled, head, legs, and arms limp, downward.

All the way down, until he at last lay only meters from the entrance to the cavern where Anij waited with the last of the Ba'ku.

"I suspect it won't be long before the drones get here," Picard called to Worf. They turned and headed quickly back to the cave, passing Beverly Crusher, who had stopped to kneel in the dust beside the wounded Son'a. The male officer lay spread-eagle, motionless except for the pronounced up-and-down movement of his rib cage. Unconscious, his face seemed even more masklike than those of other Son'a Picard had seen, the pale skin pulled so taut that his open mouth did not gape, but opened in a millimeters-wide slit. Around the edges of his face, especially at the jawline, was the festering crust of all those of his race.

With professional intensity, Crusher lifted her tricorder and scanned her patient; at the readout, her head drew back sharply, slightly.

She did not look up from it. "Captain . . ."

Picard moved cautiously to her as she proffered him the tricorder. "Look at this medscan."

He took it from her, studied it briefly. At first glance, he saw nothing surprising. He had seen this readout before himself, didn't understand what Beverly was talking about. It was perfectly normal for—

And then he stopped himself, looked down at the unconscious Son'a, at Beverly, whose expression was one of grim confirmation, then back at the readout.

This was a normal readout *for a Ba'ku*. But the man who lay in front of them was Son'a. The captain gazed back at Crusher. "How could this be possible?"

Crusher gave a little disbelieving shake of her head that set her copper hair swinging, and looked over her shoulder at the cavern exit, where Anij and Tournel were busy organizing the last group of Ba'ku for departure. "Maybe we should ask them."

Inside the exit cavern that led to escape, dozens of Ba'ku blocked Artim's vision so that he did not see the wounding of the Son'a; but he had heard the ear-splitting force of the Klingon's weapon, had heard the landslide, had heard the murmurs of his elders reporting what had happened.

Up to that moment, Artim, sweating from the moist heat, water up to his ankles, bare toes squishing smooth mud, had managed to calm himself despite the teeth-chattering explosions that never stopped. Everyone with him was an adult; all the other children had already been moved. But Artim had refused: as the village leader's son, he felt obliged to stay and help Tournel and Anij—both of whom had ignored his offer and told him to stay out of the way as they readied each group for departure.

Now, they were readying the very last group. The boy pressed against the warm, damp stone wall and briefly closed his eyes in revulsion. He had known all along that the Starfleet officers were firing weapons— but he had convinced himself that they were more deterrents than anything else, or perhaps some sort of protective devices.

Was it right for Picard to hurt the Son'a back? In the context of the quiet Ba'ku village, listening to his

elders talk about peace, Artim could easily understand the senselessness of all violence. But he had
never before faced an unprovoked attack. Right now,
the Son'a were acting as if they wanted to kill the
remaining Ba'ku.

Did it make sense for Artim and all the others to
give up, to die for the sake of peace?

Is he dead? Is he dead? Is he dead?

The murmur moved quickly through the crowd.
Tournel answered, and was echoed.

I don't know. . . . I don't know. . . .

*No, wait, he's alive . . . Alive . . . Alive . . . The
healer is with him. She is helping him. . . .*

Artim breathed a sigh of relief, then opened his
eyes, just as Anij said quickly, "It is time." At once,
she and Tournel organized the group into six pairs,
and began filing them, two at a time, through the gap
in the wall out into the day. Artim was in the final
pair; and slowly, as they approached the burned-away
wall, he could see more and more of what lay outside:
Captain Picard and the burly, intimidating creature
called a Klingon . . . the listless Son'a . . . and at last,
Data and the beautiful dark-haired officer returning.

At the sight of the android, Artim smiled with
relief. Artificial Data might be, but there was a
constancy to him, a gentleness that reminded the boy
of his father, Sojef . . . and *that* caused Artim to fight
back tears of uncertainty and sorrow.

Don't be a baby. Data promised you that Father was someplace safe, Artim reminded himself; he did not consider that, if the Son'a were now desperate enough to try killing the Ba'ku here on the ground, they might—

Don't even think it.

Data could be trusted, and that was that. And the other Ba'ku—especially Anij, the closest thing Artim had to a mother—seemed to trust all of the Starfleet officers, especially the brave Captain Picard.

Did that mean they all now agreed that weapons were okay? Artim sighed; grown-ups were sometimes a mystery. As he neared the opening in the wall, he absently gave his pocket a gentle pat . . .

. . . and started as he realized it was empty. His palm pet had run away.

With a low cry that was swallowed up by a series of overhead explosions, Artim rushed back into the belly of the cavern.

Anij, meantime, was working hard to ignore the overhead blasts that made the bones in her head vibrate, made the earth beneath her feet tremble, made silt from the cavern ceiling float down and settle on her head, in her eyes. Working hard, as well, not to choke on the dust stirred up by the constant explosions or the landslide that brought the Son'a down. She forced her focus to remain on the last group of her people to make a run for the higher caverns—at least, *most* of her focus was on the group while she quickly checked her row of refugees, with Tournel doing the same to his row. But as she helped here to tighten a backpack, there to soothe an animal, some of her thoughts were with Jean-Luc Picard, and the danger he faced on her people's behalf; other thoughts were with Sojef.

After all the centuries, all the questions, she had finally learned one thing: she was not in love with Sojef, had never been. She respected him, esteemed him, loved him as a friend; indeed, was now terribly worried about what had happened to him. . . .

But her heart belonged to an offlander. Ba'ku wisdom taught that romantic love was a joy restricted to a very few, that most should content themselves with a marriage based on friendship. But Anij had experienced that joy now, that passion, and would settle for nothing less.

Even so, she was mature enough to know that Picard was too restless to settle among the Ba'ku; and that she did not have it in her heart to leave her people. Surely he would have to leave, and she stay . . . yet the fact made no difference in the way she felt.

And the bravery both Jean-Luc and Sojef had shown inspired her. Anij had always been cool, level-headed during emergencies, which was one reason she was an unofficial leader; now she worked especially hard to show calmness, to reassure.

Again, the ground beneath her shuddered, and an overhead explosion rattled her bones; she ignored it and began counting the number of Ba'ku in her row. There were fourteen of them remaining now, including herself and Tournel, which meant that, without the leaders in front, there should be twelve people, six pairs. Six in her row, and she counted silently to herself as she stood back to review them.

One, two, three, four, five. . . .

Only five, yet there were six in Tournel's row, where a terra-cotta–haired woman stood alone, unpaired, at the end of the line, all her belongings rolled up inside a single exquisite patchwork spread. This was Da'nea, unwed, opinionated, and a brilliant quilt artist; normally, Anij welcomed conversation with her; now, she could only ask (without appearing too frightened): "Is that everyone?"

Da'nea's head jerked up suddenly as she registered her friend's question; like most of the others, she had been utterly distracted by the sights and sounds of what was going on outside. She looked at the unoccupied space beside her, then, panicked, said: "Artim . . ."

Artim, Anij realized, with a thrill of dread. She loved the boy as her son; and if Sojef survived this, she would never be able to face him again if she let his only child perish.

She absorbed her immediate surroundings with a sweeping glance, then clutched Da'nea's upper arm. "Wait here."

She knew Artim well—well enough to know that only one thing would cause him to disobey his elders, to do something this foolish—and so she spun about and ran back, back through the narrow, muddy corridors beneath the now ominously shaking ceiling to the large room where they had first taken refuge.

And there was Artim, on his knees as he scooped up his palm pet from the damp ground, then held his open hand level with his nose and smiled at the little creature.

"Artim!" Anij snapped, with more anger than the boy had ever heard in her tone. He turned to regard her owlishly, clearly unaware of the crime he had just committed. But there was no time for pity or explanations; she seized his arm and dragged him along with her.

Overhead, the ceiling rumbled frighteningly; a cascade of pebbles spilled down, grazing Anij's shoulder. Collapse would occur in a matter of seconds now. *For the boy's sake,* she prayed. *For the boy's sake, let us make it out in time. . . .*

Picard was gasping by the time he and his away team made it back down to the cavern exit, where Tournel waited with the last evacuation group.

Anij was not there.

The realization pierced Picard like a plasma beam; the dread he felt must have clearly shown, for Tournel said, the instant the captain stepped into earshot: "Anij went to find Artim."

A distant voice, muted by thick cavern walls, called from inside: "I've got him!"

Anij. Through sheer will, Picard hid the deep surge of relief that ran through him at the knowledge she was alive; at the same time, he felt dread upon learning *where* she was. Upon returning from higher ground, he could see the aerial attacks as he—and Data, Crusher, Worf, Troi—approached the cavern where the last of the Ba'ku remained. The roof was on the verge of giving way, reducing the whole structure to a heap of rubble; the captain had arrived intending to make sure that *everyone* was out of the cave.

Upon hearing Anij's voice, Picard acted without an instant's thought, without the reflection that might have made him choose Data instead for such a dangerous rescue mission; at the sound of her voice, he ran, so quickly that those remaining behind had no opportunity to dissuade him. So quickly, that within a matter of two heartbeats, he met her and Artim in the corridor that led to the largest part of the cavern. She was literally pushing the boy ahead of her, forcing him to run faster as pebbles rained down from the ceiling.

And then the mountainside where the cavern rested took a direct hit; Picard heard it at the same time Anij did, and technophobe or no, she knew exactly what it meant. The ground swelled like an ocean wave, then settled, while above them, there came the roar of solid rock separating, falling. . . .

At that very instant, he looked at her, and she at him. Their shared gaze could have lasted only a millisecond, no more, yet to Picard it seemed timeless. A silence overtook him, one in which the noisy chaos surrounding them receded abruptly, and for that moment, there was nothing in the world at all save Anij.

No fear, no defeat in her shining eyes: only love and gratitude toward him, a real joy that he had shared in her life. He drew in a breath at the beauty of those eyes, all apprehension toward death vanished. If he was to die, let it be here, now, in the company of this amazing woman; surely he had loved no one better, and his one hope was that she could read that in his own gaze.

And then the roar and dust and stones intruded; coughing, Picard caught the boy Artim by the arm and flung him, reeling, out of the cave. He turned back and stretched a hand toward Anij, who was reaching back toward him.

Reaching, reaching . . .

A stone struck the back of his head; he dropped

groaning to his knees, then looked up, only to find that the hail of rocks was so thick now, Anij had disappeared from sight. Another rock struck his shoulder, then his kidneys, then his whole back, forcing him facedown into the mud. Through effort, he managed to get onto his side and breathe, but by then the rocks kept coming, coming, until his lungs were full of dust and he felt himself spinning down into darkness. . . .

Picard's final shove sent the boy Artim hurtling forward, forced to run to the exit or fall facedown into the slippery mud. Artim ran—narrow chest heaving with gasps that were very close to sobs. Around him, behind him, the world was collapsing in a deafening hailstorm of stone. He dared not glance over his shoulder at those following, concerned though he was; if his father was alive, then it was Artim's duty to remain so as well.

Abruptly, the boy stumbled through the opening, and Data's strong arms caught Artim's thin ones. With astonishing ease, the android pulled the boy away from the danger. At the sight of Data's steady, placid expression, Artim felt a surge of relief; that relief vanished at once when the boy turned to see the devastation he had left behind.

The mouth of the cave had collapsed into a heap of

rubble—and left no trace of the two people who had come to save him.

"Anij!" Artim screamed with real anguish. She had risked her life for his . . . and so had Captain Picard. How could he live if they both were dead? And if Anij and Father were both gone . . . ?

Data gently turned the boy about to speak to him. Artim braced himself to hear the typical grown-up lie: that Anij would be all right, that he should not worry. . . .

How can she be all right with all those stones crushing her?

But in Data there were no lies, no condescension. He bent down so that his straightforward amber eyes were on a level with Artim's own, and said in a tone firm but considerate: "Tournel will take you the rest of the way."

Artim's first impulse was to scream again, to weep, to plead; but in the face of Data's calm, the boy summoned his own fledgling self-control. He looked over at Tournel and the group, all of whom stared aghast at the collapsed cavern, dust streaming outward from it like smoke.

Already the other Starfleet officers were preparing a rescue operation. One of them, a dark-skinned man with strange bony growths on his forehead (rather like the hide of an *i'choto* lizard, Artim decided), pressed a button on his chest and boomed, in his gruff voice: "Worf to Picard."

Beside him, the red-haired healer held up a black box and reported, "Two lifesigns. One extremely faint . . ."

Two lives. Artim's heart fluttered. *Anij is alive, and the captain, too. . . .*

Still, he couldn't leave at that moment, not until he saw Anij for himself. Besides, he felt safest with Data. Data told him the truth, and even the Son'a, with all their weapons, couldn't defeat the android.

"No," Artim told Data at last. "I want to stay with you." At the same time, he heard the childish petulance in his own tone and was embarrassed.

The android was entirely unmoved. "It is safer there. I will join you shortly."

Behind them, the beautiful dark-haired woman was looking down at her own black box. "There are almost four metric tons of rock blocking our way. . . ." She drew a weapon, the same one Captain Picard had fired at the Son'a, and pointed it at the rocks.

At once, the bony-browed man put his large hand on her wrist. "That might cause another cave-in."

Artim turned away, sighing; Data was, as always, right. Obediently, the boy took the last place in line in Tournel's group; immediately, the group began to run. Somehow, Artim managed to keep his balance while glancing back over his shoulder, at the sight of the four Starfleet officers digging desperately through the rocky ruins. . . .

Blackness. Pain.

Pain in his head, in his neck, in his back. Pain from a thousand bruises, a dozen cuts. He moaned softly, and even that slight movement of his lips and jaw caused a fresh jolt of agony to move down his left cheek, from eye to chin.

It was tempting to slip back into unconsciousness and escape the misery . . . tempting, except for one thing.

"Anij . . ."

He cried her name out hoarsely, using the pain itself like a lifeline to pull himself back to full consciousness. With both arms, he reached out, groping for her in the darkness, touching nothing but silt and rubble.

"Worf to Picard . . ."

How many times had the Klingon patiently called for him? Several, the captain realized, but this was the first he had registered. "Yes," he called, hearing the weakness in his own voice. He cleared his throat, tried again, this time a little stronger. "Yes, I can hear you. . . ."

"We're trying to get to you, sir." In the background, Picard heard the thud of rocks against earth.

With a groan, he pushed himself from his side onto his knees, causing a small landslide as soil and rocks, none of them smaller than a fist, rolled off him. The ground, an uneven landscape now of rocky shards, was hardly hospitable to his palms and knees, but he gritted his teeth and persisted, testing arms and legs: nothing broken. Outside of the bruises, what felt like a mild concussion, and the painful cut on his cheek, he was in fair shape—and extremely lucky. Yet the blow to his head had disoriented him somewhat: he had been running toward Anij, reaching for her, and she for him. Picard remembered waking up on his side, but where was she now in relation to him? His surroundings were now unrecognizable heaps of silt, pebbles, boulders, jagged monoliths of stone; he dared not guess which way he had come.

He chose what seemed like the likeliest direction, and crawled forward a ginger half-step, then paused as his movement caused the stones and pebbles beneath him to shift and scatter. The interior of the collapsed cavern was dark as a moonless night, but as his eyes slowly adjusted, he sensed that a large slab of the ceiling had come down in one piece, and wedged itself atop a large pile of rocks so that he had been protected from being crushed by it. As best he could tell it was stable—for the moment—and so he continued his slow search, his heart and mind numbed to all possibilities but one: that he would find Anij, find her alive and well.

Had it not been for the dark purple of her robe, he

might not have noticed her at all, surrounded by a pearl gray cairn of stones, so pale was her skin . . . as pale as the blond curls that lay fanned about her head. Gray-white, Picard thought at first sight of her face, like a waning moon—but he reassured himself that everything in such darkness was painted in shades of gray.

"Anij," he said urgently. She would open her eyes now, smile, and sit up. She would speak and reassure him. Never mind that she was lying there so motionless, so limp.

In the dreadful silence that followed, her eyelids twitched, fluttered gently open for a heartbeat to look at him—long enough to reveal eyes the same dull whitish gray, all starlight extinguished. By then, he had found his tricorder still on his belt and trained it on her with trembling hands.

Massive internal bleeding. She was in shock and could die at any moment.

"Help is coming," he said, with a faint, reassuring smile; he got the heart-wrenching impression that she recognized him and was trying to smile back, but it was beyond her strength. Her dimmed eyes closed with a slow and terrible finality.

Picard pressed his combadge. "Worf, you must *hurry. . . .*"

"We can't risk using phasers, sir," the Klingon's voice replied.

Of course, of course; the ruins were too unstable. Silently cursing the situation, Picard replied, "I understand. Tell Doctor Crusher to have a hypospray of lectrazine ready. . . ."

Beverly Crusher's voice, now, filled with both professional and personal compassion, not only for her patient—but for her friend, Jean-Luc, as well. *So she knows,* Picard realized, *how I feel about Anij. Perhaps the whole crew knows.* . . . "How bad is she, Captain?"

He fought to keep the emotion from his tone, and did not quite succeed. "I'm losing her."

"We're coming as fast as we can," Crusher said, with a resoluteness that made him silently bless her.

Picard reached down for Anij's hand—so cool now, and limp—and lifted it to his cheek. He had always envied the Vulcans for their longer lifespans, and had never quite fathomed why they seemed to regret the deaths of their elders so greatly. Surely the great tragedy lay in the deaths of the younger, in the unused potential. A 250-year-old being had enjoyed a full, useful lifespan, and those around him or her should be ready to let that being go.

Before he had met Anij and the Ba'ku, he had always thought that after two centuries or so, one would become bored with life, would know all that there was to know. But now he understood. Anij was so vital, so alive, such a treasure of accumulated maturity, insight, and knowledge, that her accidental

214

death seemed no less than a crime of nature. Age had made her more valuable, not less so.

He pressed her hand more firmly to his cheek, and with all the intensity of will and heart that was in him, told her:

"Stay with me. Don't let go of this moment, Anij. Help me find the power to make you live in this moment. . . ."

Her eyelids fluttered, then remained one quarter open; she meant, he knew, to look on him once more before dying. But that he would not permit.

"Just one more moment," he whispered. "And then one more after that . . . and one more after that. . . ."

As Picard held her gaze, it seemed he could hear her very heartbeat, and the breath in her lungs, both growing slower, calmer, stronger, merging with the sound of his own. He heard the gentle sweep of her eyelashes as she blinked, then widened her eyes slightly. In her eyes, he saw a glimmer of radiance, and watched it grow, merging with his own inner light until the darkness surrounding them eased and the airborne dust, descending softly and slowly as snowflakes around them, glittered diamond-bright. And in that moment, there were no Son'a, no Ba'ku, no struggles, no death, no danger, no fear, no *Enterprise;* there were only Anij, and himself, and the light.

How long that endless moment lasted, he could not say, but it was broken by the sudden sharp intrusion of sunlight. Beverly Crusher suddenly appeared on Anij's other side and emptied a hypospray into the Ba'ku woman's neck, then ran a tricorder over her. The doctor smiled over at Picard. "She's stabilizing."

Squinting as his eyes adjusted to the light, the captain nodded with relief. "Is it safe to move her?"

"Safer than leaving her in here."

Aches and bruises forgotten, Picard balanced himself on one foot and one knee, then lifted Anij into his arms and began to follow Crusher out of the collapsed cavern. On the way, Anij spoke weakly, but Picard heard the teasing undercurrent.

"And you thought it would take centuries to learn . . ."

He could only smile down at her with genuine affection.

The far end of the cavern, where Worf had burned an escape exit into the calcite, was still standing; and as the group—Worf, Troi, Data, Crusher, accompanied by the captain and Anij—stepped out into the open air, Picard's sense of timelessness was replaced by urgent immediacy.

Agleam with sunlight, five silver drones hovered trembling like hummingbirds in the air, blocking the path to the mountain caverns. Waiting.

There was no time for reflection, no point in returning to what remained of the collapsed cavern for shelter. As if linked by a group mind, the officers immediately took battle positions, shoulder-to-shoulder, an arm's breadth apart, and drew their weapons. Picard gently lay Anij upon the ground, then straightened to catch the phaser rifle pitched him by Worf. The captain went down on one knee in front of her, his body a shield.

Abruptly, the drones gave birth, quicksilver hives spewing forth armies of tiny, barbed insects.

The air filled with phaser fire, some of it generated by Picard. He remained motionless, determined to protect Anij as best he could; he was aware of Worf nearby, ducking and rolling to miss a hail of small projectiles, of Troi dropping and firing from the ground.

One, two swift drones destroyed in a fleeting ruby blaze; the captain could not have said whose phaser fire was responsible. The third one he hit neatly, cleanly, before it could fire again. More firing, and at last the fourth was destroyed, leaving only one. . . .

The last drone fired, launching another shining swarm—this one directed squarely at the captain and his ward.

Picard fired instantly, creating a significant gap in the center of the group, but it was not enough. The sound of small projectiles whizzed past his ears; he looked down at Anij, and to his horror saw the tiny metal tag protruding from her shoulder . . .

. . . less than a second before he felt the sting in his own side, and saw the barb sticking out of his jacket.

Desperately, he tried to pull the tag from her shoulder, but it would not give, and he found himself staring into her startled eyes as the world around them began to glimmer, shift, and dissolve. . . .

ELEVEN
☆

It was Sojef who greeted them first, inside the massive brig that was so comfortably appointed Picard knew at once he was aboard a Son'a vessel. Some eighty Ba'ku were quietly seated on the thickly padded floor, some with children nestled in their laps; clearly, Sojef had taken charge of the situation, quickly reuniting families and comforting those who had been separated from their loved ones.

As for the Ba'ku leader's own concerns, he kept those hidden until he was seated facing Picard, with his back turned to his people; only then did the absolute calm on his features, in his voice, waver as he asked: "Artim . . . Do you know what has become of him, Captain?"

Anij answered from where she lay between the two men, her head propped up on Picard's thigh; she lacked the strength to sit up on her own, and her voice was weak, though determined. "Your son is well, Sojef. Data—the artificial life-form—is taking excellent care of him now. And Jean-Luc himself saved him from great danger when the cave collapsed."

Picard smoothed her hair. "You're forgetting, Anij. *You* were the one who went back for the boy. . . ."

"My gratitude to you both," Sojef said, with forced evenness; abruptly, his voice dropped to a near-whisper. "And *you,*" he said to Anij. "You have been injured because of this?"

Picard nodded on her behalf.

Sojef did not lift his gaze from the wounded woman's face. "And seriously so," he told her, with utter frankness. "Will you survive?"

The captain opened his mouth to reply . . . then closed it as he caught a glance of Sojef's expression. There was compassion there, and the concern of a very old, very dear friend. . . .

And something much more. For an instant, Picard felt something akin to guilt; it passed and was replaced by pity. Sojef was obviously in love with Anij, and had been for—how long? Centuries? It must have been enormously difficult for him to see another man, an offlander no less, stroking her hair.

"I'll live," Anij answered, smiling back at the Ba'ku

leader with more platonic, but no less genuine, affection, at the same instant Picard said:

"She was bleeding internally. We stopped that, and she'll survive without further treatment, but it would be best for her—"

He broke off, suddenly aware that the background hum of a force field, as well as the gentle murmurs of Ba'ku voices, had ceased. He followed the others' gazes toward the brig entry, where Subahdar Gallatin, whom Picard recognized from the "rescue" of those on the Ba'ku planet, escorted Dougherty into the brig.

The admiral appeared ravaged. Physically, he was the same: tall and straight of stature, silver-haired, lean . . . but only the body was unchanged. The essence of the man—the confidence, the directness, the near-palpable mental intensity and will that marked a Starfleet admiral, especially one as respected as Matthew Dougherty—had fled.

Dougherty entered the brig, scanning every face; he was looking for the captain, of course, but Picard found himself too overwhelmed by loathing to call out, to hasten short the inevitable. Instead, he wound one protective arm around Anij, and with the other stroked her hair, until at last the admiral spotted him and made his way over, accompanied by the silent, expressionless Gallatin.

Dougherty looked down sternly at the trio on the floor; Picard returned his gaze with such repressed rage he was surprised the sheer emotional force of it did not knock Dougherty from his feet. It did, however, cause the admiral to avert his eyes for half a heartbeat, but he rallied himself and said firmly:

"Order them to surrender, and I promise you won't be court-martialed."

It was a pale imitation of the old Dougherty: there was nothing behind the gruff tone, the hard glare, the attempt at authority, but a lost man.

Despite Picard's effort at control, the corner of his mouth curled in disgust. "If court-martial is the only way to tell the people of the Federation what happened here, then I welcome it."

Dougherty blinked, cleared his throat, briefly looked over at the uniformed (albeit subtly for a Son'a) Gallatin as if seeking an answer; but the subahdar merely held his gaze steadily. Clearly, the admiral had had no plan to deal with Picard beyond this, and was now at an impasse.

Time to choose, Admiral. Me and the Ba'ku, or the Son'a.

Suddenly Dougherty was spared: there came murmurs in the brig, then the rising and scattering of Ba'ku as the ahdar, Ru'afo, came storming in, furred and feathered robes swinging, a padd clutched in one pale-knuckled hand. He ignored those surrounding him, stepping in the midst of or directly onto the sitting prisoners, until he came face to face with

Dougherty. The Son'a commander seemed to notice no one else in the room—not even Picard.

"The *Enterprise* has destroyed one of my ships," Ru'afo hissed, his voice low and trembling with rage. "The other is on fire, requesting assistance." He shoved the padd in front of the admiral's nose; Dougherty seemed to deflate ever so slightly.

"The *Enterprise* would only fire if she were defending herself," Picard told the besieged Dougherty. "Ru'afo must have ordered an attack." He paused. "I can't believe he would have given that order without your consent, Admiral."

The older man stared at him then—apparently with the intent of silencing Picard with a stern look. But Picard's words had clearly hit their mark; Dougherty was too proud to let himself look away, but his eyes went hollow; and Picard, sickened to see the truth so confirmed, said softly:

"I wonder which of us will be facing that court-martial. . . ."

The admiral turned heavily away, and said to Ru'afo in a dulled voice, "There's nothing further to be gained from this."

"You're right," the ahdar replied with quiet vicious glee. "This is going to end now." He turned to Picard, for the first time acknowledging the captain's presence. "The Ba'ku want to stay on the planet. Let them. I'm going to launch the injector."

Except for Ru'afo's, every other face in the group went slack-jawed with horror—including, Picard noticed through his own dismay, the face of the sedately dressed Gallatin. The subahdar composed his features at once, but not before Picard caught his gaze. As if ashamed, Gallatin looked away . . . but the captain already had learned an extremely important fact: All aboard the Son'a ship were not in total agreement regarding the fate of the Ba'ku. It made sense: Gallatin had been hidden in the duck blind for weeks, had been watching and remembering family and old friends; and there was a compassion in him that the ahdar seemed entirely to lack.

Dougherty spoke first, and in his indignant voice and words, Picard heard the admiral he had known. "You're not going to launch *anything* until—"

"In six hours," Ru'afo countered, in a tone of even greater authority, "every living thing in this system will be dead or dying." He turned, again with a flourish of fur and feathers, and strode toward the exit, sending Ba'ku scurrying out of his way.

Again, there was something in his demeanor that struck a chord of memory in Picard: he felt as though he knew Ru'afo—and Ru'afo's yearning for revenge—intimately, knew also that the ahdar would make good on his threat unless something could be done to stop him.

Picard called softly after him. "You would kill your

own people, Ru'afo? Your own parents, your brothers, sisters . . ." At Dougherty's sharp astonishment, he added, "Didn't you know, Admiral? The Ba'ku and the Son'a are the same race."

The admiral turned in amazement to Ru'afo, who had stopped and half turned; the Son'a would not return Dougherty's questioning gaze, and his mouth and jaw twitched with hatred when Sojef rose and stepped forward to face him. Clearly, Ru'afo feared splitting his newly repaired skin again, for he seemed to be struggling hard to keep anger from contorting his features.

"Picard just told us . . . our DNA is the same. Which one were you?" Sojef asked gently, compassionately. "Gal'na? Ro'tin? Belath'nin . . . ?"

Ru'afo's voice was cold, his eyes narrow with contempt. "Those names, those children, are gone forever."

"What is he talking about?" Dougherty demanded, honestly astonished.

Sojef turned to him to explain. "A century ago, a group of our young people wanted to follow the ways of the offlanders. They tried to take over the colony, and when they failed—"

"When we failed," Ru'afo said poisonously, "you exiled us. To die slowly."

In Picard's arms, Anij stirred and raised her head. "You're Ro'tin, aren't you . . . ?" she asked; the Son'a

225

leader's silence was confirmation enough. "There's something in the voice." She turned next to regard the subahdar. "Would you be his friend, Gal'na?"

The officer looked away, clearly pained.

"I helped your mother bathe you when you were a child," Anij reminded him, her tone fond and faraway, from a lyrical, happier time. "She still speaks of you."

To Dougherty, Picard said, "You've brought the Federation into the middle of a blood feud, Admiral. The children have returned to expel their elders, just as they were once expelled. Except Ru'afo's need for revenge has now escalated to parricide."

At that, the ahdar emitted a small hiss, then turned and left without further comment—due to the vain fear, Picard suspected, that if he remained another instant he would lose his temper and again damage his stretched, brittle complexion.

Gallatin turned to follow, then paused, and cast a final, reluctant glance at Sojef before following the outraged Ru'afo.

Dougherty remained behind, a soul in tatters, staring first at Sojef, then down at Picard with a transparent need for forgiveness. "It was for the Federation," the admiral said numbly. "It was all for the Federation. . . ."

Yet even Picard could see that the admiral was deluding himself; there had been something far deep-

226

er, far more personal at stake; but he said nothing to Dougherty. There was nothing more *to* say. It was up to the admiral now to redeem himself . . . or remain in his own personal hell.

He and the Ba'ku watched as Dougherty turned and silently, heavily followed the same path Ru'afo and Gallatin had taken out of the brig. Picard looked down at Anij and heard the hum of a force field leaping back into place, and the receding sound of a slow, even footfall. . . .

For Matthew Dougherty, it was a very long walk through the spacious corridors of the Son'a vessel.

He had not lied to Picard, he told himself; he *had* done it for the Federation. For every sentient being who had suffered and died in the Federation, and that included Madalyn. He still could not see so much the harm in relocating these people in order to grant the galaxy healing, youth, virtual immortality . . . but harming them was unconscionable. What he had done in allowing Ru'afo's ships to go after the *Enterprise* was unconscionable; more than a thousand people, and he had been willing to allow them to be exterminated. Why had it been so easy?

Because they had been distant. Because he knew he would not have to witness the destruction firsthand. It was cleaner, neater that way . . . easier to kill.

Would he have felt that way about relocating the

Ba'ku if he had first lived among them, gotten to know them as people instead of simply observing their culture as an intellectual exercise?

He sighed, and noticed that he had instinctively headed toward the Son'a bridge. A quick check there showed Gallatin, but no one knew where the ahdar had gone. Dougherty wandered back out into the corridor and let instinct be his guide.

The fact was, Ru'afo had never intended to deal honestly with him, the Ba'ku, or the Federation. . . . Indeed, with every step, it became clearer and clearer to the admiral that Ru'afo would never share the life-giving properties of the Ba'ku planet with anyone but the Son'a.

Grief and weakness, Dougherty realized, had made him easy prey. Had made him listen to Ru'afo's glib reassurances without considering the Ba'ku's point of view, made him champion the Son'a's cause, made him convince the Federation Council to support it. How, so late, could he now make amends?

Chances were that he could not. He was a lone Starfleet officer aboard a ship of Son'a with extremely sophisticated weaponry and an agenda that was now the opposite of his. Even so, he was morally bound—

by whatever shred of ethics I have left

—to try to stop what was happening.

He let go a deep breath and felt a wave of repressed self-revulsion, a burden carried for months, leave him; at once, he felt lighter, more serene. Decisiveness, which had eluded him for just as long, returned.

He knew precisely what he would say to Ru'afo; he also had the realistic understanding that the ahdar would react with increased rage. But he was willing to risk it—willing, at the moment, to risk everything for a chance at redemption.

He found himself standing at the entrance to the body sculpture chamber. If Ru'afo had been serious about deploying the collector, then all personnel would be on duty, and the chamber should be deserted. But Dougherty's instinct told him it was not entirely so.

He drew a breath and stepped inside the spacious structure. Indeed, not a single Elloran attendant greeted him, and the individual treatment booths were dim and deserted—all but one, where Ru'afo sat, eyes closed, face still creased with anger, in front of a device that bathed his features in green, pulsating light. *A living, rotting corpse,* Dougherty thought.

Slowly, deliberately, the admiral walked over to him and stood at his elbow. The Son'a clearly heard, for his body involuntarily tensed; but he kept his eyes closed, refusing to acknowledge Dougherty's presence.

"We're taking this ship out of here," Dougherty said, and meant it. "This mission is over."

Ru'afo's eyes and mouth opened narrowly. "It is *not* over."

"It is *over,*" Dougherty insisted. And he turned to move away, to go to the bridge and give the commands that would take them out of the Briar Patch, into communication range with Starfleet.

But before he could do so, Ru'afo rose, seized him by the shoulders, and with brute force moved him backward. Dougherty resisted, but Ru'afo was the larger man, and was possessed of startling, overwhelming strength.

"I do not take orders from you!" the ahdar roared.

With equal fury, Dougherty shouted back, "If you launch the injector while the planet is still populated, the Federation will pursue you until—"

He broke off, air pushed from his lungs as Ru'afo slammed him down into one of the treatment chairs, then forced his head into a face-lifting device.

"The Federation," Ru'afo said, sneering, "will never know what happened here."

And in the split second before the Son'a hit the controls, Matthew Dougherty realized that he was going to die: not later, in the brig with Picard and the Ba'ku, or after a period of house arrest, but *now,* this moment.

And something very curious happened. Although his body struggled wildly, thrashing so hard that

Ru'afo had to exert considerable force to hold him down, the admiral's consciousness calmed at once; indeed, observed the goings-on like a disinterested spectator.

The device pulled his ears upward first, in the face-lift procedure he had seen carried out on Ru'afo so many times—stretching, stretching, until at last he felt his skin begin to tear; and then there was pain, terrible pain as the device pushed and pulled, first breaking his nose and then crushing his jaw, and finally his skull, with deafening crunches.

Yet observer Dougherty remained preternaturally calm. This was certainly a horrible death, as deaths went, and yet . . . the realization of what was happening to him brought with it a sense of relief and release far deeper than the one he had experienced moments before. The suffering itself was a bad thing, surely, but it was only temporary, transitory; death itself was an unutterably peaceful, freeing event.

At the same time, he felt mild regret that he should have to leave Picard to face this alone. He would have liked to have helped them, after all he had done to harm them; but there was nothing he could do now, nothing but wish them all well and let them go. . . .

As for his body, his head and neck were now so contorted that his trachea was crushed, and his limbs had stopped their thrashing and now simply trembled.

Even that ceased as anoxia took hold, and whatever consciousness remained in his body dimmed, then darkened forever.

Yet his observer self had more clarity than ever; and as he looked about himself he realized it was no longer Ru'afo who stood over him, hovering . . .

But Madalyn, Madalyn with her swinging silver hair and dimples, grinning down at him, saying, *See? Who says dying is such a terrible thing?*

He reached up for her, smiling.

TWELVE

☆

On the Son'a bridge, Gallatin sat in the ahdar's chair overseeing a full complement of crew—Son'a, Tarlac, Elloran. To an outside observer, the scene was ostensibly calm: officers working silently at their stations, the subahdar sitting, arms folded, staring blankly at the viewscreen, where the Ba'ku planet—with the radiation collector in place—rotated lazily behind a gossamer veil of glittering cosmic dust.

Inside, Gallatin seethed. Not with anger alone—although there was enough of that, directed not only at himself but at Ru'afo, and at the Starfleet captain who had forced them to take such desperate measures.

He had never meant it to come this far, had never meant for anyone to be hurt. He had only wanted to be what temperament and talent had urged him to be—a scientist—but he had had the misfortune to be born into a community that feared the very thing he loved.

As a child, he had asked many questions. At first they were answered honestly and directly; over time, they were discouraged, and when in his youth he discovered a hidden treasure trove of cultural and scientific history in the caves—all on computer—he swore to devote his life to refining the exquisite technology of his ancestors.

For months, he secretly traveled to the cave and slowly unraveled the secrets of the computer, and his forebears. Someone in the community, one of the original immigrants—he never discovered who—had decided to leave a complete record of the world from which he or she had come.

His ancestors called themselves the Ka'bu (and the pacifistic dissenters made a linguistic play on the name by reversing the consonants to call themselves the Ba'ku, which meant "the Peaceful"). The Ka'bu had traveled the galaxy in sophisticated space vessels; they had lived elegantly, in the pursuit of beauty, art, and physical perfection, relying on mechanization to do their labor for them, insteading of sweating out in the fields in coarse homespun. But the artist class had separated from the warrior class, and squabbling began—that class separation, Gallatin (then Gal'na) had decided, caused their downfall . . . *not* the availability of weapons.

His mother had taught him the importance of honesty, especially self-honesty; so it was that Gal'na could not bear the realization that his elders had eschewed science—which by its own nature was truth itself—in its entirety.

What was inherently evil about spaceships? Gal'na had asked Sojef one day, and was frustrated by the calm reply:

There is no evil in the vessels themselves—but in the **attitude** *that spawns the vessels. Technology is a weed: once it takes root, it strangles all other philosophies, all other ways of doing things. It cannot be controlled: once our culture embraced it, it had to accept both the good and the bad truths it brings. The good aspect of technology helped to heal our ancestors; the bad, to destroy them. Here the world itself heals us. We have the good; what need have we of the bad?*

Gal'na had a thousand logical replies: *We don't have to make their same mistake. We can learn from them. Why should we not be free to travel? To live more comfortable lifestyles?*

But he kept silent, for he had heard the subtext in Sojef's apparently logical explanation: fear. The Ba'ku who had experienced the Wars had been terrified for their lives, and that terror made them completely reject something that was neither bad nor good in itself, but neutral.

So Gal'na observed his friends closely, discovered who in the village was curious, even interested, in reviving the old technology and science: all of them were younger, second-generation. None had lived on the original home planet; all had escaped the Wars.

Many agreed with Gal'na—especially Ro'tin, a young farmer with an athlete's strength and grace. Ro'tin also had a gift for leadership: he often spoke out on behalf of the younger generation at village meetings. Some said Sojef should consider training him as a second-in-command instead of the young Tournel, but others felt that his occasional temperamental outbursts made him unfit.

Gal'na's technological vision and genius impressed Ro'tin deeply; he immediately befriended the young scientist and became the unofficial organizer of the Science Movement. This relieved the shy Gal'na, who was much more at ease with computers and numbers than rhetoric; when at last the Son'a demanded a leader, Gal'na insisted the right fall to Ro'tin.

By then, they had taken on new names, taken from Ka'bu historical records; they were Gallatin now, and Ru'afo, and inseparable friends, each in awe of the other's talent. Ru'afo ruthlessly guarded the more sensitive Gallatin's research time, and received public censure from the elders for barring them from inspecting Gallatin's laboratory.

In time, the Son'a group grew so large that Ru'afo and Gallatin went to Sojef and announced a takeover. A peaceable one, of course, they added pointedly, quick to prove that their exposure to technology had not tainted their ethics.

The leader of the Ba'ku countered that such a thing would be fair only if it represented a majority: heady with confidence, Ru'afo agreed, and so the villagers were polled.

The loss was crushing—in terms of both numbers and emotional effect upon the two disgraced Son'a leaders. Consensus of the loyal Ba'ku doomed the Son'a to exile . . . not from the village, but from the planet itself; word had leaked out long ago that the Son'a were in the process of constructing a spaceship out in the desert, a ship large enough to carry all eighty of them.

If you change your hearts, you are welcome to return, Sojef had said, without a trace of animosity. Indeed, there had been only sorrow in his eyes, and the eyes of every remaining villager.

Never, Gallatin had vowed, his own heart poisoned with hate by such a betrayal. Could they not see how fear controlled them? Why could they not listen to him? Why send him away, from his own people, his own village, for something that was not a crime?

Some months later, when the ship was at last completed, the Son'a left. Far from easing, the hatred only increased over time: for it was over time that Gallatin and the others began to understand the full impact of their exile.

They had been doomed to age, and then die.

Youthful, feeling immortal when they left, they had never considered such a fate until it began to strike them: skin that slowly lost its tautness, jaws once firm that began to sag, hair that grayed or fell out altogether, teeth that chipped and yellowed. Bones and joints, once reliable, began to creak and ache, and—the worst of all horrors—disease born of aging struck unpredictably. This was a hell they had never known, had never seen their parents experience; indeed, the time came at last when they realized that they were older than the elders they had left behind.

At the first signs of decrepitude, they had taken extreme measures to reverse the aging process: had engaged in Gallatin's attempt to mimic the unique form of radiation encountered on the Ba'ku planet. It had left them sterile, unable to bear children, to experience even that limited form of immortality. . . .

In his fury, Gallatin had designed the collector— which guaranteed that the Ba'ku would share in the misery of exile. Perhaps he might have found a way, given several more months of research, to collect the unique metaphasic radiation that encircled his home planet without destroying the latter; but at the time, he was interested only in justice. The Ba'ku would know, as he had, the pain of homesickness; would know, as he had, the horrors of aging.

But he would not condemn them to die, as they had him. He would show them that he was morally superior, after all; the healing properties of their planet would be gathered and distributed freely throughout the Federation.

And when he was young again, healthy again, he would confront Sojef and show the elder how wrong he had been, all those decades ago.

Now, Ru'afo's threat echoed in Gallatin's mind as the subahdar stared at the viewscreen. He understood how Ru'afo felt; over the years, as death approached them all, it only seemed more and more appropriate that the Ba'ku received the same penalty they had meted out to their children.

But Gallatin had never meant to kill them—had never dreamed of it—and Ru'afo's suggestion that they simply activate the collector and destroy everyone down on the planet surface ate at his, Gallatin's, soul.

After a hundred years, he had sat among them; his own aunt had offered him food and failed to recognize him. He had seen his mother playing with a young child in the distance, and wondered: might that be his brother? He had felt their warmth and acceptance, regardless of the fact that he was a rebel, a Son'a, a spy . . . and he considered the last one hundred years of his life and found them lacking.

True, the Ba'ku were wrong about technology; but Gallatin had been surprised by how very *right* they were about so much else.

The bridge doors slid open; Ru'afo entered, hands folded stiffly behind his back, eyes peculiarly bright. Gallatin rose as the ahdar stepped up to him and said, "Admiral Dougherty will not be joining us for dinner."

The forced lightness in his tone sent a wave of nausea washing over Gallatin; the admiral, an intelligent, gracious man by Gallatin's standards, was no doubt dead, murdered by the ahdar's own hands. *Ah, Ro'tin, what have we become?*

Continuing, Ru'afo said, "Deploy the collector." And at his second-in-command's hesitation, his voice hardened. "Do you have a problem with those orders?"

"May I talk to you alone?" Gallatin asked, his voice polite, low.

Ru'afo looked beyond him, at the next Son'a in command, Ra'eb, and ordered loudly, "Deploy the collector!"

Ra'eb complied at once, while, with Ru'afo in tow, Gallatin moved out of earshot of the others. "Moving them is one thing," the subahdar said softly. *"Killing* them all—"

He had braced himself for another display of Ru'afo's temper, which had grown increasingly violent of late; to his surprise, the ahdar replied with perfect calm. "No one hated them more than you, Gal'na." He paused, then added gently, "We've come a long way together. This is the moment we've planned for so many years. . . ." He laid a reassuring hand on Gallatin's shoulder.

The subahdar released a silent sigh. In the past, Ru'afo had always supported him and his research, had served as friend and mentor a thousand times over, even though Gallatin had never necessarily approved of Ru'afo's ethics. In his youth, perhaps, he had even admired Ru'afo's boldness in flouting laws and ethics, as proof that the Ba'ku elders and their old-fashioned morals no longer had any hold on the Son'a. Up to the present, Gallatin had gone along with everything his friend had ordered. But now . . .

"Separate the Starfleet personnel and secure them in the aft cargo hold," Ru'afo ordered, his tone low and amicable. "See that Picard joins them."

Shock upon shock. Dully, Gallatin replied, "The shields in that section won't protect them against the thermolytic reaction. . . ."

"Thank you for reminding me," Ru'afo said with a small smile and settled into his chair.

For a moment, Gallatin lingered at his commander's elbow and watched as the scene on the viewer shifted from that of the planet to the Son'a science vessel. Massive hatches on her flank opened and gave birth to a long cylinder, which parted slowly down the middle, a poisonous flower blooming.

Before the collector could fully deploy, Gallatin turned and left—not because he was in any hurry to carry out Ru'afo's orders, but because he knew the deployment stages all too well. For years, he had poured all his energy—all his love and hate—into designing and creating the device, and into creating the simulation that Ru'afo spent endless hours watching.

Now Gallatin could not bear to see it in reality. But even as he exited the bridge and headed down the corridor, he saw it in his mind's eye: brilliant solar sails unfurling like a newborn butterfly's wings, expanding in front of the planet's rings, gleaming.

So beautiful, and so deadly . . .

Back in the brig, Picard stood on the strong backs of two kneeling Ba'ku and examined the force field generators tucked under a ceiling panel. They were Son'a in design, not Federation, and therefore both simpler and more sophisticated; at the moment, the captain was puzzling over the power source, which was far from obvious. Once he found it, an even greater puzzle would present itself: how to sabotage Ru'afo's plans. . . .

"Jean-Luc," Anij hissed suddenly.

Approaching footsteps outside. Picard immediately slipped the ceiling panel back into place and hopped off his supporters, who turned and sat cross-legged on the floor as if they'd been doing so for hours. For people who prided themselves on total honesty, the captain noted, the Ba'ku were doing a marvelous job of dissembling in front of their Son'a captors.

The force-field hum ceased abruptly as Picard moved to Anij's side; Subahdar Gallatin stood at the brig entry, plasma weapon aimed directly at the Starfleet captain.

"Come with me," the Son'a said.

At first glance, his expression and tone conveyed nothing more than a soldier doing his duty; but as Picard studied him, he saw deeper signs of the same pain he had seen on Gallatin's face when Ru'afo had threatened to destroy all those on the Ba'ku planet.

Picard was no fool: Ru'afo was now making good on his threat, and to both divert and test his second-in-command, the ahdar had ordered Gallatin to execute Picard. The Son'a could not risk Starfleet's interference; and if Matthew Dougherty was not already dead, he soon would be.

Picard glanced down at Anij, whose pale eyes were wide with concern that verged on panic; she was no fool either, and clearly understood why Gallatin had come. But Picard tried to communicate in one smile a wealth of information:

Don't worry. Of all the Son'a, he is the most unsure of Ru'afo's decision. . . . And without inside help, the captain had little chance of averting the coming destruction.

Anij must have sensed some of his confidence, for she managed a faint smile before he turned and exited the brig. Keeping his weapon trained on his prisoner, Gallatin touched a bulkhead control; the force field leapt back into place.

The Son'a motioned with his weapon, keeping Picard a pace ahead of him. Again, the captain sensed no hostility, no hatred from Gallatin, only an overwhelming sense of reluctance and even an attitude of courtesy toward his victim.

Cautiously, gently, Picard at last spoke. "It must have been strange for you." He gave a sidewise, backward glance and caught the curious tilt of Gallatin's head. "When you were a hostage. Surrounded by all the friends and families you knew so many years ago. All of them looking exactly as they did. Almost like looking through the eyes of childhood again."

They stopped at a pair of lift doors; as Gallatin

pressed the control, Picard turned and fixed his gaze upon him with sudden intensity.

"And here you are trying to *close* those eyes . . . trying not to see what the bitterness has done to your people . . . how it's turned Ru'afo into a madman . . . and to you." The captain paused. "It's turned you into a coward."

The subahdar jerked his chin sharply at that, but Picard persisted. "A man who denies his conscience."

The lift arrived silently; the doors slid open with a whisper. "Get in," Gallatin said evenly, and in his cool composure Picard saw a childhood of training among the Ba'ku.

Picard entered, turned to face the doors; Gallatin moved to enter, but as he stepped onto the threshold, Picard said with venom:

"A coward . . . without the moral courage to prevent an atrocity. You *offend* me."

The Son'a's eyes widened with incredulity. "Is this how a Federation officer pleads for his life?" Anger crept into his tone; but there was also a glimmer of humor.

"I'm not pleading for my life," Picard said, with utter sincerity. "I'm pleading for yours." He paused. "You can still go home, Gal'na."

Silhouetted in the entryway, Gallatin's form seemed ever so slightly to sag; at the same time, he let go a sigh that was almost a groan, that contained the misery of over a century. At last, he stepped inside the lift.

"Computer. Close turbolift doors."

The doors slid closed behind him as he lowered his weapon; for the first time, Picard looked upon an aged Son'a face and saw there a Ba'ku. Clearly, Gallatin had never intended to carry out an execution; but it was also clear that he was at a loss as to how to free himself and those he loved from destruction.

"What you're asking me to do," Gallatin said softly, "is impossible."

Picard wasted no time. "Do you know how to disable the injector?"

The Son'a's eyes flickered briefly, as if he found something comical in Picard's question; but the brightness dimmed immediately. Somberly, he nodded. "But I would need to be on the bridge. The crew is loyal to Ru'afo. An assault would fail—"

"Perhaps we could lure him away."

This time, the Son'a shook his head. "It doesn't matter where he is. As soon as he realizes something is happening, he'll override my commands with one word to his comlink."

Picard considered this a moment. He had not come this far, risked this much, to fail. There *had* to be a solution, and as he willed his mind to retrieve one, he flashed upon a memory: rowing across the lake, climbing with Data into the holoship and discovering a perfect holographic replica of the Ba'ku village. . . .

"What if he *doesn't* realize something's happening," he said excitedly. Gallatin drew back, confused, but Picard persisted. "Can you get me to a transmitter? I have to speak with Worf and Data on the surface. We'll need their help."

"Deck twelve," Gallatin told the lift computer. To Picard, he gave a slow, single nod; and with that solitary gesture, the captain felt a renewed surge of hope.

Enchanted, Ru'afo watched the viewscreen as the collector glided, majestic as an airborne raptor, toward its intended prey. With solar sails spread wide, the collector was elegant in design, even beautiful—as beautiful, Ru'afo thought, as the justice it was about to dispense. Gallatin had always been as much artist as scientist . . . though, given his way, he never would have allowed his device to kill the Ba'ku; he had never broken fully with them in his heart.

Ru'afo had always known of this weakness; even so, he loved Gallatin as a brother and stood in awe of his talents. Indeed, he would always respect Gallatin as the originator of the Son'a movement . . . even if the subahdar lacked the ability to lead. That was Ru'afo's forte; he had always taken care to spare Gallatin the more upsetting aspects of particular missions, encouraging him instead to work on new projects . . . especially *this* project, the metaphasic radiation collector.

But now the time had come for Gallatin to face the truth: that Ru'afo had never intended to share the metaphasic radiation with the Federation, had worked with them only in order to facilitate its collection. Dougherty had been a dead man the instant he set foot on the Son'a ship, and the sanctimonious Captain Picard was an excuse to take drastic action.

The Federation people disgusted him, all of them; all their highly touted technology, and all these centuries of gathering the work of some of the galaxy's best scientists, and *still* they had not conquered old age and death. Ru'afo had wanted to shake both Picard and Dougherty, with their morality and their rules, and scream: *How can you bear it? Death is staring us in the face, could strike us down at any moment; all of us know the indignity and pain of lost youth. Why are you wasting time talking about morality, about regulations?*

Sheep. Sheep, waiting to die; but such was not Ru'afo's birthright, and he would fight death with every scrap of his power, intelligence, will.

And he had been waiting a long time to exact the proper revenge on the elders who had expelled the

Son'a: death, the same death they had wished on their children, slow and agonizing.

Every one of those elders sat now in the Son'a brig: and every one of them would be told of the total destruction of their world, their remaining loved ones, before they were put to death.

It was only fair. And Gallatin would have to accept it, as graciously as he had just accepted escorting Picard to his doom.

Exhilarated by the thought, by the sight on the viewscreen, Ru'afo ordered: "Initiate separation protocols."

"Activating injector assembly," the Tarlac ensign— what *was* his name? Ru'afo could never remember— replied.

At the adjoining station, a young Elloran officer added: "Separation in three minutes."

Ru'afo glanced at the chronometer at his station and saw the countdown begin; at the same time, he felt his heartbeat quicken, though outwardly he remained as calm and determined as a Ba'ku.

A seasoned Son'a lieutenant, Lutonin, scowled down at his monitor. "A small craft is coming up from the surface," he reported. "It's powering up its weapons."

Had Ru'afo been able to lift his brows any higher, he would have then. "On screen."

The glorious scene of the sailing collector vanished and was replaced by an annoying sight: a tiny Federation vessel, the one Picard had taken down to the planet surface. Ru'afo clicked his tongue in disgust.

"One person aboard," Lutonin reported. "It's the android."

Ru'afo waved a dismissive hand; compared to the vast Son'a ship, the Federation vessel was scarcely larger than a microbe. "He's no threat."

At that moment, the ship shuddered slightly; there came the muted rumble of a weak attack.

Following behind Gallatin, Picard crawled through the narrow passageway filled with electrical conduits and circuitry. He would have loved to stop and examine them—they were neater, more compact than those aboard the *Enterprise*—but there was no time.

"Data to Picard."

The captain started slightly at the sound, even though the comlink had been preset to low volume; Picard answered in a near whisper. "Yes, Data . . ."

"Sir, they're ignoring my attack."

The unpleasant possibility had occurred to Picard, but Gallatin had earlier reassured him that persistence would pay off . . . and at the moment, he had no choice but to trust the subahdar. "Keep firing tachyon bursts into their shield grid," the captain ordered. "Is Worf in position?"

"Yes, sir. He's ready for simultaneous transport."

In the dimness, Gallatin turned back and signaled over his shoulder for silence.

"We're approaching the bridge now," the captain whispered. "Picard out. . . ." He drew in a breath and prayed that he had read Gallatin correctly, and he was not about to be betrayed. . . .

"Separation in one minute," the Elloran said.

Ru'afo felt his heart beat in time with each passing second. Rapt, he stared at the collector sailing regally toward its destination.

Gal'na, Gal'na, see what beauty you have wrought! Perhaps he should have let Gallatin remain on the bridge, share in this moment of glory. . . . But instinct told Ru'afo that his old friend would not be able to bear it; that the ensuing argument between them would shake the confidence of the bridge crew, seeing the two most revered Son'a at odds.

No, the time would come when they would stand together, young and strong as they once were; then, Gallatin would thank him. Then, Gallatin would understand. . . .

"Sir," Lutonin said sharply, "the Federation ship is creating a disruption in our shields."

The Son'a lieutenant beside him nodded in agreement. "If the shields go out of phase, it will increase our exposure to the thermolytic reaction."

Ru'afo withdrew from his reverie, irritated. "Very well. Destroy that ship and reset our shield harmonics. Do *not* delay the countdown. . . ."

In the cockpit aboard the captain's yacht, Data sat calmly as a nova-brilliant blast of plasma sent the small ship spinning out of control. He maintained his orientation and attempted to manipulate the console—

—until a second burst caused the console to erupt into sparks, which dimmed and were quickly replaced by smoke. Clearly, some of the controls were inactive, and it would take a second or two to determine whether they could be rerouted so the ship could be safely landed.

But that point was moot for the time being; at that instant, his most important function was to inform Picard of his success, in time for the captain and his Son'a assistant to take the immediate and appropriate action. . . .

"Data to Picard," he intoned, as the streams of smoke enveloped the console, the cockpit, the yacht; all three were beginning to glow dull red with the heat, as was the android himself. "They are rotating the shield harmonics. I am attempting to return to the surface."

No reply. He had not expected one, and so he set

about working to stabilize the ship, which was still hurtling planetward. . . .

"The Federation ship has been disabled," the nameless Tarlac reported, in a tone of mild relief.

"Separation in twenty seconds," the Elloran added, and Ru'afo felt a thrill that left gooseflesh on the worn, tired skin of his arms. The horror and indignity of death and aging receded, replaced by the approach of life and beautiful youth . . . so close, Ru'afo felt a rise in his spirits, in his energy, as if he were already reborn.

A sudden shimmer, a flash. Ru'afo blinked as his vision blurred, then cleared again. "What was that?"

Lutonin, first to check his monitor, shook his head. "I don't know. Systems don't seem affected."

"Separation in ten seconds," the Elloran droned. Ru'afo verified it with a check of his chronometer, again feeling his heart beat with the passage of each unit of time.

"Five seconds . . ."

They passed in an eternity; they passed in the twinkling of an eye. At last, the collector drew close to the planet's shimmering rainbow rings and glided to a halt. A small elliptical object emerged from its center and hurtled toward one of the rings.

"Injector assembly has separated," the Tarlac

said—unnecessarily, for Ru'afo had already committed the sequence to memory, so well that it permeated his dreams. To see it now in reality was an overwhelming experience, one that stirred up waves of shifting emotion: joy, satisfaction, the pain of old hurts never healed, rage. It was for Ru'afo pure art, a deeply moving metaphor for past wrongs righted.

Before him, the injector pierced the first prismatically radiant ring, and immediately dispersed a series of charges, white-hot novas within the rainbows that made Ru'afo wince with pain; they had not been so bright in the simulation. Determination kept his eyes open, and when the afterimage cleared, he saw a sight that left him on the precipice of tears.

Flumes of particulate matter, which had reflected light—in essence, the ring itself—began to scatter, like volatile vapors rising in the sun. Within a second, no more, the first ring had dissolved, and the next had begun.

On the planet surface, the radiation levels would be rising . . . and the people would just now be starting to die.

Mesmerized by the vision on the screen, Ru'afo let go a breath of pure awe. "Exactly as the simulations predicted . . ."

He heard rather than saw the Son'a ensign, Frenil, say with concerned confusion, "Sir, I'm not showing any change in metaphasic flux levels."

Irritated by this interruption during such a hallowed moment, Ru'afo frowned, but never took his gaze from the viewscreen. "Your scanners must be malfunctioning."

A pause; then Frenil spoke again, his tone a key higher with puzzlement. "All ship functions are off-line."

Ru'afo turned at that. Frenil was intelligent, trustworthy—but the ahdar refused to believe him at that moment, simply because Ru'afo could not permit the possibility of anything going wrong. Not now, after a century of waiting . . .

He went immediately to the nearest station and checked the readouts for himself. Frenil could not be right, could *not* be right, but there it was, the impossible: ship functions were off-line. His tone rose with panicked anger.

"How can there be no ship functions if the viewscreen is working, artificial gravity is stable, life support is—"

Ru'afo broke off as something in the periphery of his vision caught his eye—something small, something subtle. He turned and moved toward it slowly, reluctant to discover what he already knew, what he could not bear to permit himself even to think. . . .

Above an unmanned console sat a small, steel gray tile that contrasted with the surrounding bulkhead. There was something familiar about that tile, something horrifyingly so: Ru'afo had seen many such tiles when Gallatin had shown him the interior of the holoship that would take the Ba'ku from their homeworld. Gallatin had taken great pride in constructing an exact duplicate of the village square, but had fretted when he discovered a small gap in the projection.

Don't worry, Ru'afo had told him then. *By the time any of them notice, it will be too late.*

Now, Ru'afo reached out and touched the tile above the console; he withdrew his fingers as if scalded, and whispered: "A holodeck?"

To the horror of the others, he pulled a disruptor from his belt and fired at the wall.

The familiar sight of his bridge dissolved, replaced by scarred gray tiles.

"A *holodeck?*"

He fired again and again, revealing more of the familiar gray grid, while his stunned officers watched. Impossible, impossible: How could this possibly have happened? Dougherty was dead, and Picard in a holding cell. . . .

Ru'afo flashed suddenly on his last encounter with Gallatin; on the uncertainty in his friend's voice and eyes. He had been too focused on what was to come to truly register Gallatin's unease; he remembered putting an encouraging hand on the subahdar's shoulder, giving him the order to escort Picard.

And he had expected—with good reason—Gallatin to comply. As long as Gallatin himself was not required to kill directly, he had always done as Ru'afo ordered; oh, he might protest from time to time, but in the end, he always obeyed. It was easier for him to let someone else make the decision, someone else take the blame.

That bastard Picard—somehow, during that short walk, he had turned Gallatin against the Son'a . . . or perhaps captured him, forced the information from him—

No, no. Gallatin might have been reluctant to kill, but he was not afraid to die.

Gal'na, Gal'na, how could you betray me on the eve of our victory?

With a roar, Ru'afo continued firing, until the hologrid gave way to a short flight of upward-leading stairs. He dashed up them, while the others followed; immediately, he stopped short.

This was Gallatin's holoship bridge, no more than a cockpit with a huge viewscreen that revealed a heart-wrenching sight: the Ba'ku planet nestled inside its glowing, perfectly intact rings.

And nearby, the metaphasic radiation collector, stalled and impotent, its injector assembly un-launched. In the foreground Ru'afo's own dark, sleek ship remained in orbit.

Gasps, as each officer caught sight of the viewscreen, followed by a beat of silence. When Ru'afo at last could speak, his voice was choked, halting.

"We were transported to the holoship when we reset our shields. Everything we saw . . . was an illusion." He hit his comlink and forced a more commanding tone. "Ru'afo, authorization delta two-one. Override all interlink commands to injector assembly."

He would not give up; *could* not, after a century of waiting, hoping. But the response of his ship's computer filled him again with frustrated rage:

"Unable to comply. Injector assembly one has been deactivated."

Aboard the real Son'a bridge, meanwhile, Picard and Gallatin waited for Worf to look up from his console.

Gallatin's conscience had saved the day, Picard realized, and so had an enormous element of luck: he had not realized that the subahdar was also the designer of the injector—and of the ship. Had the captain sought help from a less knowledgeable Son'a, the Ba'ku on the planet would never have survived; as it was, the chronometer countdown was frozen at 00:06.

Uncomfortably close, but Picard had not permitted himself to consider the death of the Ba'ku—especially that of Anij—for an instant, lest it interfere with his efficiency; now that the danger was over, the realization of how very close Ru'afo had come to succeeding left the captain slightly shaken.

Gallatin himself had obviously made the right decision; he seemed deeply relieved and at peace— even a bit younger, as if years had been erased along with guilt. At any rate, he appeared quite a different man from the one who had escorted Picard from the brig.

At last, Worf glanced up from his monitor and reported, "All injector subsystems are confirmed off-line."

Picard and Gallatin smiled faintly at each other. "Decloak the holoship and engage a tractor beam, Mister Worf," the captain ordered.

The Klingon complied by pressing several panels. On the viewscreen, the smaller holoship appeared abruptly. Right about now, Picard decided, Ru'afo and crew were realizing that their own attempt at deceit had been used against them.

The thought cheered him in a most ungracious way; he put it aside. "Gal'na," he requested, "open a channel to Commander Data."

The Son'a did so with uncanny speed, then nodded at Picard.

"Data?" the captain asked.

He could hear, on the other end of the comlink, the sounds of the captain's yacht shaking apart; indeed, before the android replied, there came a terrible shrieking sound of metal tearing.

"Precarious, sir," Data said calmly. "I am having trouble re-entering the atmosphere."

It was then that Picard detected the subtler sound of licking flames; the image of the ship—and Data—glowing red-hot came to him unbidden.

"Understood," the captain said swiftly. "Well done."

At the hum of the transporter, Picard severed the connection.

"And well done to you," he said, smiling, and turned to Gallatin, only to find the Son'a's expression darkening. He paused. "What is it, Gallatin? What's wrong?"

"Ru'afo." The subahdar lifted his somber face toward the viewscreen, where his holoship creation, entrapped by the tractor beam, orbited alongside the much larger Son'a vessel. "Don't say *well done* quite yet, Captain. It isn't over."

Picard drew back. "Is there something we've forgotten? Some way Ru'afo could—"

Gallatin shook his head. "He's secure; there's no way he can beam here from the holoship—of that I'm sure. But I know *him* . . . have known him, for many years. This will only make him more determined than ever to fight, to succeed. If there *is* a way to escape and ignite the rings, Ru'afo will find it. He's a very dangerous man."

Picard followed his grim gaze to the holoship, but turned as Worf said, with deadpan voice and expression:

"He sounds very much like *you,* sir."

THIRTEEN

——————— ☆ ———————

Ru'afo forced himself to look away from the too-painful sight of the stalled collector; instead, he stared over the shoulder of the Tarlac, who stood awaiting orders at the single basic console.

The solution to his, Ru'afo's, frustration lay somewhere in these controls; and bitter as he was at that moment toward Gallatin, he was also deeply grateful for Gallatin's past willingness to explain his designs, to educate Ru'afo thoroughly in every detail of their use. And Ru'afo had been an eager student, in part because he sincerely admired his friend's talent—but also because, as ahdar, he needed such knowledge, had used it a thousand times over to save himself and his crew from their disgruntled victims.

Gallatin may have been the technological genius, but Ru'afo was a brilliant strategist with a talent for finding answers where there were none. Now, though he stared down at the console over his officer's shoulder, he saw not the stripped-down controls, but instead Gallatin.

Gallatin, in the ship's hangar against the cavernous spiny backdrop of the collector's interior, climbing the rungs upward with the energy and enthusiasm of Gal'na the child, motioning for his friend Ro'tin to follow. How long ago had it been? Two years ago? Three? Compared to the size of the subahdar's newest creation, they were arthropods within a giant web.

And Ru'afo had followed, wheezing, old bones complaining as he crawled up the skeletal support structure behind Gallatin the jubilant, who gestured grandly about him.

"The sails will be stored where we're climbing now. And up there"—he pointed—"is where I'll be putting the ignition matrix for the injector assembly. Once ignited, the injector will launch and detonate within the rings, causing the chain reaction we spoke about."

He had smiled then, the sudden, dazzling smile of childhood, and Ru'afo could not help but grin back, despite the toll taken on his overstretched skin. Youth seemed a tangible thing, within his grasp; and for an

263

instant, the two of them were not the aged, tired creatures time had made them, but the strong, terribly beautiful young men who had challenged their elders a century before.

Ru'afo had forced the smile from his lips. He dared not celebrate yet—not when there was the specter of an untimely death for either of them before their immortality was assured. Time now to work, to consider all possibilities. He climbed to Gallatin's level and faced him, panting, clinging to the rungs. Sweat dripped into his eyes, but the height was dizzying, and he dared not loosen the grip of even one hand to wipe it away. "What safeguards are you planning on putting in place?"

"Safeguards?" Gallatin regarded him blankly.

"To ensure detonation, in case there are problems with the launch. It is, after all, unmanned, isn't it?"

With a nod, the subahdar had allowed that it was— and proceeded to explain all the remote methods by which any such problems could be solved. But the look in Gallatin's eye—that distant, faraway gaze that said he was looking inward, not outward—told Ru'afo that the scientist in him had been challenged.

And he had not been surprised when, days later, Gallatin had come to him and explained that he was going to equip the collector's interior with life support and its own internal control console, in case of an emergency.

"As a last resort, in case some type of manual problem comes up. If need be, I could beam over and make any adjustment. . . ." He proceeded to explain how even the injector assembly would have its own control panel, which would have its own cockpit, and, of course, the special antimetaphasic shields. They required their own separate energy source, which meant more time redesigning the assembly, but since they were adding the cockpit anyway—

"Stop," Ru'afo had said. Two decades had passed since he and Gallatin had vowed to find a way to take the metaphasic radiation from the Ba'ku, and ten years since Gallatin had drafted his first design. The Son'a had aged horribly during that time. "Too much, too much—you'll spend another year playing with *that.* Just leave the control panel as it is and put a force field around it. We haven't time."

Gallatin had frowned—not out of anger, but puzzlement, as his scientist's mind considered the notion. "But the metaphasic shields are going to require a redesign anyway. A cockpit won't take as much time—"

"Then put a regular force field around it."

Gallatin had scowled in earnest then. "Ru'afo . . . no one could survive the metaphasic radiation long enough to come back. It'd be a suicide mission."

"Then we'll send an Elloran or a Tarlac. Could they survive long enough to provide a simple task?"

"Yes, but—"

"Perfect." Smiling, Ru'afo had put a hand on his friend's shoulder—just as he had today, in the minutes before Gallatin's betrayal—and said heartily, "Thanks to you, Gallatin, we will not fail. . . ."

Now, in the present, looking over the Tarlac's shoulder, Ru'afo gave a grim, inward smile and uttered silently: *Thanks to you, Gallatin, I will not fail. . . .*

To the Tarlac, he said, "This ship is equipped with fourteen long-range transporters. Are they *all* useless?"

The officer rapidly worked the console, then glanced unhappily up at his commander. "They must have been locked and secured after we were beamed here."

Ru'afo paused no more than an instant. "Isolate one and reroute its command sequence through the auxiliary processor."

Behind him, Lutonin protested cautiously, "Sir . . . there's nothing we can do. They already have control of our ship."

Normally, such direct disagreement from any but Gallatin would have provoked Ru'afo's fury—but he held himself in check, limiting himself instead to the thought that Lutonin was a coward and a fool to think that the six of them could not outsmart two Starfleet officers and one Son'a—even if that Son'a was Gallatin. Instead he turned and held Lutonin with a pointed look.

"I don't plan on going back to our ship."

Aboard the partially repaired bridge of the *Enterprise,* Will Riker sat at command, stroking his smooth chin and staring at the viewscreen, with its colorful display of swirling debris and gases. They had entered the Briar Patch hours earlier—for Riker, a nearly unbearable stretch of time, since communications with the away team had been impossible.

If the Son'a had been so willing to destroy the *Enterprise* and all aboard her, what was to keep them from slaughtering those on the Ba'ku planet's surface?

The thought had plagued him from the moment the *Enterprise* escaped her pursuers—especially as regarded Deanna. Certainly, he was deeply concerned about the captain and crew . . . but the thoughts that kept him from sleep, that permeated his waking hours, were of Deanna—Deanna on the day they first had met, Deanna teasing him in the library, Deanna laughing, skin wet and shining amid the bubbles.

The fact was that he was as deeply in love with her as he had ever been. He'd been certain those feelings were simply part of the Briar Patch's rejuvenation effect, the stirring up of the hormones of youth; but once the ship was clear of the Patch, the intensity of his feelings did not alter. In truth, by the time he informed Starfleet Command of the real situation between the Ba'ku and the Son'a, his love and concern for her had increased—not faded, as he had expected.

Nor was this the wild, immature infatuation of youth. When he first had met her, he had fallen in love with an image of her, a projection of what he had secretly desired, what he had thought the perfect woman should be: someone who wanted exactly what he wanted, someone whose thoughts were identical to his, someone who always understood everything he said exactly the way he'd intended it. And it was the discrepancy between that image and Deanna herself that had caused much of their conflict.

Now, he wanted only the woman herself, with all her quirks, imperfections, beauty, and strength; he wanted to be a part of her life, experience her, learn from her. And he wanted it, this time, to last.

But if he had lost her now . . .

His reverie was interrupted by Lieutenant Daniels, who called from tactical: "Commander, we're within sensor range of the Son'a ship. I'm picking up on Captain Picard's biosignature on board."

Riker swiveled in his chair to stare at Daniels with a

mixture of surprise and relief. Picard was alive, which was excellent news. "Establish communications, Mister Daniels."

"Enterprise to Picard."

At the sound of his second-in-command's voice, Picard smiled with delight as he pressed the Son'a companel; behind him, Worf glanced up briefly from his console with a faintly upbeat look that, for the Klingon, served as an expression of pure exultation. Even Gallatin seemed pleased. "Number One."

"We should be at your position within an hour," Riker's disembodied voice said. "Do you need assistance?"

"Negative," Picard replied, feeling a hint of pride at the fact. "Did you succeed?"

Riker paused ever so fleetingly, as if anticipating the effect his words would have. "The council has ordered a halt to the Ba'ku relocation while they conduct a top-level review."

"Top-level review, my ass," Picard flared, infuriated. "There'll be no cover-up of this. Not after I get—"

"Captain," Worf interrupted; the concern in his voice made Picard break off and look over at him immediately.

The Klingon gestured at the chronometer display, which had been frozen at 00:06. Impossibly, it was counting down again; as Picard watched, aghast, the numbers flickered, then changed from 02:56 to 02:55.

At once, Gallatin bent over the console he was sitting at and furiously worked the controls, then looked up again at his Starfleet companions. "The separation protocols have been reset on board the collector. I can't override."

"Scan for lifesigns," Picard told Worf quickly.

The Klingon complied, then answered: "One. It's Ru'afo."

"Can you beam him off?"

Worf shook his head. "Negative, sir. He's raised shields."

"Is there any other way to disable the injector?" Picard turned to the Son'a.

"Perhaps," Gallatin said. His tone, far from despairing, was instead sharp, focused: this was a man, Picard realized, who was as disciplined as any officer in the fleet, who was setting his mind toward finding a solution rather than giving up.

And he was Ru'afo's second-in-command, which meant that the ahdar was a formidable foe, indeed.

Within a heartbeat, Gallatin motioned them toward the display on his monitor—that of the metaphasic radiation collector. He zoomed in on the section called the injector assembly, the part he had worked so hard to disarm . . . and which Ru'afo was now attempting to relaunch.

"If we could get onto the collector, we could remove the ignition matrix"—the subahdar pointed a gnarled finger at a half-meter-square panel of circuitry connected to a larger conduit—"directly from the injector assembly." Here he indicated a shuttle-sized object.

While he spoke, Worf checked his readouts. "Sir, there's a small opening in the shields at the base of the coupling adapter. I might be able to beam through it. . . ."

Picard walked over to the Klingon's station and peered over Worf's shoulder. Overlaid over the collector's schematics was a highlighted area some two hundred meters to the side of and below the injector. The captain glanced up quickly at the chronometer.

02:31.

True, as a Klingon, Worf was more powerful, able to climb the distance faster than Picard; but the captain would not risk another's life unless it was absolutely necessary. And in this case, it was not; a human could cover the distance in plenty of time.

He frowned and nodded: *Let's do it.* But Worf misunderstood the gesture as an order, and rose, then moved in the direction of the nearest transporter pad.

Picard blocked him. "Remain at your post, Commander."

"Sir," Worf countered; it was more a question than a statement.

"Mister Worf," the captain admonished. No time for explanations, and given his rank, he did not need to give one; keenly aware of the racing chronometer, Picard strode over to the transporter, removing his jacket as he did, and asking of Gallatin: "The ignition sequence—what can you tell me?"

Gallatin rose. A wave of emotion passed over his face, and in it Picard saw determination, guilt, resolution; instinct told him the Son'a wanted very badly to take his place, to make amends by stopping the injector himself . . . yet knew that, given his aged body, he had less chance than Picard of succeeding. And realized that the captain had good reason not to trust him entirely in a face-to-face confrontation with his old friend and ahdar.

Perhaps Gallatin guessed, too, that Picard, like Ru'afo, could not be successfully argued with.

"The thrusters activate one minute before separation," Gallatin said swiftly. "You'll see the cryogenic tanks venting. Don't use any laser tools or weapons after that; they could ignite the propellant exhaust. The substructure will retract fifteen seconds prior to separation."

Picard listened, nodding, as he strapped a phaser

rifle to his chest, then stepped onto the transporter pad itself while Worf worked the controls.

02:11.

The captain watched as the Klingon and Gallatin, now both standing and gazing steadily at him with concern and hope, blurred out of focus and dissolved . . .

. . . and in place of the transporter pad beneath his feet, Picard found himself standing on a platform near the base of the sail-support structure, some hundred meters above the base of the collector itself. On Gallatin's computer display, it had appeared far neater, but now the captain saw that it was no more than a collection of metal railing, conduits, and planks—rather like a holo he'd once seen of Old Earth's Coney Island roller coaster. The interior bulkhead upon which the structure rested curved in an oddly sharp ellipse.

He took a moment to orient himself: far above and to his left was the several-decks-high injector assembly—clearly not meant for manned operation; in reality, the climb looked far more suitable for a mountaineer than it had in Gallatin's simulation. To his left on the collector floor stood Ru'afo, with his back to both Picard and the injector; the ahdar worked busily at a control panel.

"Separation in two minutes," the computer counted down overhead.

Picard caught hold of metal railing and began to climb. He could not move neatly upward, but was forced to go from railing to conduit to platform to railing; despite the danger, he dared not slow his pace. It was already going to take far more time than he had calculated to arrive at his destination.

He heard the soft bleep of an alarm beneath him. The computer warning of an intruder, he realized; Ru'afo knew now that he was here. But Picard did not slow, did not look down—he was exposed upon the railing, hands and feet both engaged, making it impossible to reach his phaser rifle. Even had he been able, the angle between the ahdar and himself made a successful return of fire unlikely.

So he climbed, counting the seconds—one, two— as if they were synchronized with the beating of his heart.

Three, four . . .

A brief flash; Picard clung to the railing and glanced down and to his left some forty meters, where a burst of plasma ricocheted off a conduit to the deck below; at the control panel, Ru'afo lowered a small handheld weapon. Its range was far less and its blast weaker than those the Son'a had used on the planet surface, a fact Picard found surprising.

But when he met Ru'afo's gaze dead on, he understood: the collector was Ru'afo's one chance at justice for his people, and harming it was unthinkable. Even at the distance of a hundred meters, the rage born of violation was all too clearly visible on the ahdar's face—a rage with which Picard was uncomfortably familiar. He, too, had once been driven by a single, mindless obsession; and in place of Ru'afo the captain saw the dark and beautiful face of Lily Sloane, Zefram Cochrane's companion from the twenty-first century, and heard the dawning revelation in her whisper:

Revenge. This is about revenge. The Borg hurt you and now you're going to hurt them back.

He had screamed at her then, with such pain and fury that his voice had broken: *The line must be drawn here—this far, and no further! I will make them pay for what they've done!*

He had been willing to risk everything for that revenge—his own life, even the lives of his crew. Lily had brought him to his senses, had made him see his hatred for what it was.

Picard felt a sudden, odd sympathy for Ru'afo: the ahdar had, after all, been born a Ba'ku. Had he so given himself over to violence he was too far gone— or was he, like Gallatin, worth saving?

A large display above the control panel flashed: 01:42. Weapon in hand, Ru'afo rushed over to the edge of the support structure and swung himself up on the nearest rung, in pursuit. Within less than a minute, Picard would be within the plasma weapon's range; the captain drew a breath and pulled himself up, faster, faster, swinging from rail to conduit until his arms and shoulders burned with the effort. No point in looking back again, and the structure offered no place to hide: his only hope lay in outracing the plasma blasts until the one-minute warning, when the vented gases made firing a weapon dangerous.

And Ru'afo dared do nothing to harm his precious collector.

So Picard climbed and counted seconds, ignoring the sweat that streamed from his brow and stung his eyes, gasping hoarsely with effort. The injector assembly became gradually closer, until, after two dozen seconds, it stood less than a handful of meters away.

A nova-bright flash: blinded, disoriented, he thought at first he had been struck, though he felt no pain; in the next instant, the plank on which he stood gave way with an eardrum-splitting snap. Through the searing yellow afterimage, he reached out, groping, and by blessed chance caught hold of a conduit. With a gymnast's grace, he swung himself, arms overhead, legs dangling, from the conduit to railing to conduit, until finally he was again able to gain a foothold.

Behind him, Ru'afo was moving faster than an aging Son'a ought; he was gaining on the captain— so much so that Picard, who was still maintaining an internal countdown, realized he would never make it to the injector assembly in time without being shot. Reluctantly, Picard seized his rifle and fired a blazing round.

The strategy worked; Ru'afo recoiled, allowing Picard to scramble the last few meters and pull himself up onto the catwalk that led to the injector. The captain sensed, rather than saw, Ru'afo behind and below him, raising the weapon again to take aim. . . .

A hiss, as the cryogenic tanks began to vent, and a low rumble as thrusters activated. Prelaunch ice, crazed and crystalline, fell away from the massive injector itself, the part of the structure which would soon be launched toward the planet rings unless Picard intervened. Overhead, the computer's impassive voice:

"One minute to separation."

The captain never slowed, never looked back; the anticipated plasma blast never came. Ru'afo's obsession with revenge had not escalated into madness, then—he was not willing to destroy himself and his dream for the sake of killing Picard. Perhaps he could still be reasoned with.

The captain ducked and held his breath as he ran past a stream of gas from the venting tanks; vapors swam in the air, causing the injector's image to waver. At last, he arrived gasping at the front of the vast injector assembly itself, where another chronometer was counting down: 00:55. In less than a heartbeat, he sized up a large panel of circuitry, firmly repressing the panic that welled in him: this looked nothing like Gallatin's display; how could he possibly find—

The ignition matrix. There in plain sight before him; he clutched it in both hands, prepared to pull it from the bulkhead with all his strength.

"Stop."

Ru'afo's voice behind him. He turned; the Son'a, red-faced and breathless, stood on the catwalk not three meters distant, plasma gun trained directly on Picard. Between them, gas vapors roiled in the air, distorting the ahdar's gape-jawed, sweating visage; from his throat came a high-pitched, reedy wheeze.

"We're getting too old for this, Ru'afo." Picard said it cautiously, but without rancor; if there was any chance of saving the ahdar—physically and emotionally—it would come now.

But the Son'a glared at him with unalloyed hate. "After today, that won't be a problem—for either of us."

His last few words were almost drowned out by the voice of the computer: "Separation in thirty seconds."

Ru'afo stretched forth his free hand, palm up, and moved his first two fingers in a commanding "come here" gesture. "Just step off the injector."

Picard eyed him in disbelief. Did the ahdar believe him to be so abysmally witless? He, Picard, was in the most strategic, protected position in the entire structure: with his hands upon the ignition matrix, behind a curtain of gas. If Ru'afo fired now, he would just as likely destroy the matrix as kill Picard. "Are you really going to risk igniting the fumes?" the captain asked, honest amusement in his voice.

Their gazes locked; Ru'afo seethed, but his hesitation acknowledged his dilemma. The captain's lips spread in a slow grin.

"No? All right. Then I will."

And Picard lifted his rifle and fired—one single shot directed point-blank at the swirling gas, some two meters above their heads.

"No!" Ru'afo shrieked, as Picard dove behind the control console.

Picard closed his eyes, but for a blazing millisecond, it was like staring wide-eyed at a daytime sun . . . then the brightness dimmed, and he peered up above the console to see the ahdar on his back on the catwalk, hood thrown back to reveal the stretched, bruised flesh stapled to the back of his skull. And then smoke began to bloom, quickly forming a thick curtain between the two men.

Immediately, Picard seized the ignition matrix and, with pure exhilaration, tore it from the wall. Regardless of what happened afterward—whether Ru'afo chose to kill him out of pure frustration, or not—Anij and Artim, Data and Troi and Crusher, and the rest of the Ba'ku, would be safe.

At once, he scrabbled downward with his prize, crawling to a plank that led him, on a lower level, back in the Son'a's direction, and he smiled to himself as he heard Ru'afo's steps above him, hurrying through the now-dissipating smoke to the injector assembly where the captain had stood only seconds before.

By the time Picard climbed back up onto the catwalk where Ru'afo had just stood, the Son'a was lifting his hand to the empty spot on the circuit board in a slow gesture of disbelief and loss.

"Looking for this?" Picard called, and raised the ignition matrix.

Ru'afo whirled about to face him. The captain braced himself for another show of rage, of vitriolic hate, of violence; and for an instant, Ru'afo's eyes were bright and terrible with such emotions.

But then the brightness dimmed. Rage was replaced by fear; hatred, by grief. These were the eyes of a man confronting his death, and the defeat of his only dream.

A loud metallic clank. The platform beneath Picard's feet shuddered slightly, then began slowly to retract from the injector assembly in preparation for launch.

For a heartbeat, Ru'afo stood frozen beside the injector's circuit board as Picard, on the catwalk, began to slide away—back into the safety of the collector's belly.

Beside the Son'a, the chronometer display on the injector control panel read 00:10. Picard watched as the ahdar caught sight of it, watched as tension seized hold of the Son'a's posture; saw, too, the sweeping glance he directed at his surroundings, and the frantic expression that came over his too-taut features as he confirmed there was no other way off the injector.

In ten seconds, Ru'afo would be launched unprotected, along with the disarmed injector, into the vacuum of space. It would be a swift death, but hardly a pleasant one, in the freezing, airless void: the silent rush of air from the lungs, the shock of immediate hypothermia.

The question remained whether the ahdar's obsession would now lead him to choose death over surrender. But if the chance existed that Ru'afo could be saved . . .

Picard set the matrix down, hurried to the very edge of the retracting catwalk, and reached out. "Take my arm!"

Already the gap between them was almost too wide: there existed only a millisecond of possibility for Ru'afo to grab hold and be pulled to safety.

But in that millisecond, Ru'afo hesitated as fear warred with hatred. In the end, panic won, and he stretched forth a mottled, bejeweled hand toward Picard's, grazing the captain's fingertips with inch-long, perfectly honed nails.

Picard strained, reaching, putting himself in a potentially precarious spot should Ru'afo catch hold; the ahdar did the same, groaning with the effort, his eyes wild and shining with tears of panic.

Yet after the first fleeting touch of nails to flesh, their hands never met, but remained inches apart, unreachably close. Thus they remained—Picard straining, palm open, fingers stretched hard apart, while Ru'afo clawed frantically, hand opening and closing like a starfish, as if the air and the growing distance between them were something palpable he might grasp.

Movement in the periphery of Picard's vision: the countdown, above and behind the ahdar's shoulder. Still the captain reached, even as he watched the inevitable.

Three.

Two.

One.

A deep rumble; the plank beneath Picard's feet

vibrated, forcing him to clutch the railing with both hands to keep from falling into the chasm. The injector separated entirely from the main structure with surprising speed, sealing Picard safely inside behind an observation window.

He expected to see Ru'afo's body hurtling past, freed from life and the constraints of gravity, and steeled himself for it; that grisly sight never came. At last he redirected his gaze at the injector, sailing harmlessly toward the Ba'ku planet's colorful rings, and was astonished to see Ru'afo, still alive beneath a force field, at the injector control panel.

Clutching the console, Ru'afo sailed aboard the injector into the magnificence of the planetary rings, separated from him only by the tragically insufficient force field.

Light and spectral color brilliant beyond torment bathed him, consumed him, permeated him until he was no longer an entity separate from it, but radiant himself from every cell, from each muscle, organ, and bone, and he cried out involuntarily at the glory and the pain.

Instinct closed his eyes. Still color and light pierced him for one heartbeat, two, three—then went utterly, irrevocably black.

The metaphasic radiation, he realized; it had blinded him. Suddenly dizzied, he sank to his knees, hands still clutching the console's edge, a penitent kneeling at the altar.

Yet in the midst of dying, he felt a sudden surge of life and put trembling fingers to his face. The top layer of skin sloughed off from their tips at once, and the sensation in them was rapidly fading, but he felt his cheeks become firmer, more supple.

He was growing younger—so swiftly that in the space of two seconds, no more, his features and skin shifted as if molten, forming and re-forming to middle age, young adulthood, youth. Death was a crucible, burning away the years.

His body shrank, became lighter, lither, and his mind freer, unsullied by hatred or fear; until he was simply the Ba'ku child Ro'tin, dying. The experience became pure and immediate, untainted by the past. Timeless . . .

Pain, as cells disintegrated, leaving blood vessels and organs to bleed. Nausea so intense it was difficult to differentiate between it and the pain. A vain effort to bring air into hemorrhaging, collapsed lungs; still growing younger, smaller, he lost his grip on the console's edge and instead leaned, gasping, against its side.

At the same time, Ro'tin felt an emotional detachment from the agonizing struggle, and a strange and exceptional clarity of thought. It was as though he were a compassionate stranger looking upon this suffering child, and he felt pity. Not because the child would die, or even so much because the child was in horrible pain; but because the child's life had been a wasted one—wasted in running from death, in fearing it, fighting it, when death meant no more than yielding to the gentle void.

And yield at last he did, letting himself fall, body, mind, and soul. . . . Into the darkness, into the silence, into a place far younger than he had ever known.

FOURTEEN

☆

In the village square, Riker squinted against the bright sun as he watched the Ba'ku, children and animals in tow, make their way down from the mountains. It was a charmingly pastoral scene—abruptly made all the lovelier by the sudden appearance of Deanna Troi alongside the rest of the away team.

Riker scarcely saw the others. Despite the stern presence of Worf beside him, he waved excitedly, as if he and Deanna had been separated years rather than days.

Like a lovesick cadet, he told himself sheepishly; it was the radiation, just the damned radiation making him act this way.

The thought was squelched immediately when Deanna caught sight of him and smiled with a radiance that took his breath away. His lips curved upward in a grin broad to the point of foolishness, yet he no longer cared, even though Worf cleared his throat nervously.

No point in trying to hide his feelings from the Klingon, Riker decided—or from anyone else, for that matter. Still holding Deanna's gaze with his own, he asked Worf:

"You think when we get away from this metaphasic radiation, it'll change the way we feel?"

A long pause, and then the Klingon replied with uncharacteristic gentleness, "Your feelings about her haven't changed since the day I met you, Commander. This place just let them out for a little fresh air."

Surprised by his friend's insightfulness, Riker turned toward him with a now-curious grin—but Worf was already moving away toward the approaching group, which included the captain.

Awkward in his fine robes, Gallatin stood upon the soft grass on the outskirts of the village square as the Ba'ku—whom, only hours ago, he had so nearly helped to kill—returned home. The younger children, fatigue already forgotten, ran ahead of their elders and dived into the golden haystacks piled neatly along the path leading to the fields.

Gallatin watched them, assailed by several emotions: joy that these children had been spared, sorrow that he had been among those who tried to harm them, loneliness that he could not simply cast off the past and join them; but his primary feeling was one of grief.

Not for the loss of the ahdar Ru'afo as he had been in his final days—at that, Gallatin felt almost shamefully relieved. But as he watched young bodies burrowing into haystacks, he grieved for the loss of his childhood friend, Ro'tin, loyal and straightforward and keenly interested in everything Gal'na had to say.

Gallatin remembered all the times he and Ro'tin had hidden from each other in the haystacks; remembered, too, that terrible day when Sojef had told them, in the presence of all the elders:

Mark these words: technology will bring about your violent downfall.

True, Gallatin thought. *Ro'tin fell to violence, as I nearly did—but Sojef was wrong.* Technology had not corrupted Ru'afo—hatred had. Picard and his people were proof that technology combined with wisdom could produce great good.

Sojef and Ro'tin had each been stubborn in his own way, and there was no reason for Gallatin to think that Sojef had changed in a century's time. Yet he, Gallatin, felt drawn to remain here; this was his home, and he knew that he could not surrender it again. But how could he live among the Ba'ku? Certainly, they had behaved hospitably toward him when they discovered the duck blind—but it had been the hospitality offered a stranger. Besides, he had been born a scientist; to deny that was to deny his own heart and mind.

How could he be himself, and still fulfill his yearning to live among his own people? Even more importantly, how could the Ba'ku accept him after all that had happened?

"I wish there were a way to bring them back home," Sojef told Picard; the two of them strolled, with Anij between them, through the village outskirts, toward the grassy meadow alongside the lake. The Ba'ku leader referred to the unawares Gallatin, whom the three of them watched.

"Ask them," Picard said. He could not clearly see Gallatin's expression from this distance, but the wistfulness in the Son'a's stance, in the cant of his head, spoke more poignantly than words could.

Anij—walking on her own now, with no more assistance than a hand resting lightly on the captain's arm—remained silent, clearly deferring to Sojef; her cautious, faintly frowning expression conveyed that this was a sore point for the Ba'ku leader.

Sojef sighed, began to speak, then stopped himself and began again. "I'm afraid there's too much bitterness . . . on both sides."

As he spoke, Picard noticed Beverly Crusher escorting a beautiful young Ba'ku woman with a long, sand-colored braid past them, toward the fields; he tried to catch the doctor's gaze, but failed. Still, he gleaned the information he wanted from the young Ba'ku's face, as she stared intently at the preoccupied Gallatin.

She was trying to recognize him, Picard knew, and failing. Until she and Crusher stood beside the Son'a, and the doctor politely signaled for his attention.

Gallatin turned, his stunned expression now in profile. Even if the woman did not know him, he immediately knew her—and at first glance, uttered a soft, solitary word.

She cried out, raised her hand to her lips, then stood on tiptoe to throw her arms about him.

For a tense instant, Gallatin stood, stiff and motionless . . . then slowly, gently, returned the embrace and leaned his head upon her shoulder.

Picard shared a knowing look with Crusher, who smiled brilliantly at him, then turned away, eager to allow the couple their privacy and to avoid a wave of sympathetic emotion.

Anij was studying the captain with an expression of dawning realization. "Mother and son," she said softly. "You arranged this?"

"I thought it might begin the healing process," Picard admitted—almost apologetically, for he had no idea whether Sojef might consider it meddling and take offense.

The Ba'ku leader considered Picard's statement in silence, then reached forth and shook the captain's hand with an expression of such deep appreciation that Picard felt overly compensated. Without a further word, Sojef strode away . . . directly toward Gallatin and his mother.

At the same instant, Worf approached with a sense of urgency. "Captain, the *Ticonderoga* has moved into orbit." That said, he turned and walked away.

When Worf had moved far away enough to grant Picard some privacy, Anij looked at him with pale eyes, and he saw his own pain at leaving reflected there. Such a wise, amazing being: she knew he loved her more than he had any other woman, and was secure in it; she also knew that he could not give up his life to remain with her.

"What am I going to do without you?" She smiled sadly as she spoke.

"I wish I could stay, but these are perilous times for the Federation," he answered in a low voice. She did

291

not need a reason, had not asked for one; he stated it aloud to convince himself more than her. "I can't abandon it to people who would threaten everything I've spent a lifetime defending. I have to go back . . . if only to slow things down at the Federation Council."

She nodded, stroking his arm to comfort him.

"But," he added, at last managing a smile, "I have three hundred and eighteen days of vacation time coming. And I intend to use them."

And Anij said, with a tone and a look he knew he would always remember, "I'll be here."

He took her into his arms and kissed her, allowing himself to slip again into timelessness. . . .

"Where's Data?" an unfamiliar man's voice said in the far distance. At the sound, Artim, immersed in a pile of faintly fragrant hay, let go his breath and popped his head up through the straw, which formed an itchy collar around his neck. He scratched it absently, peering about for his playmates and the poser of the question; not an instant later, Data's head poked through the straw beside him.

"Data!" the woman doctor called out, and Artim saw the group of Starfleet officers waiting for him in the meadow. "It's time to go!"

Artim felt a surge of sorrow. His new companion had finally mastered the concept of hide-and-seek and was turning into an amazing playmate; but Artim would miss him for a greater reason than that. Data had saved his life—but it was even more than that. He, Artim, *cared* for Data as a friend . . . cared about a collection of circuitry and positronic matrices.

And he believed, regardless of everything that his father and his society had taught him, that Data cared for him. That Data was a good *person,* which meant that all technology was not by its very nature evil.

It was something he intended to discuss at great length with his father.

Firmly squelching any impulse toward tears, Artim crawled from the hay and brushed straw from his hair, arms, and legs. Data did the same, then paused before returning to his waiting peers.

"I have to go now," he told Artim.

Artim looked down at his feet and nodded. "Bye."

"Bye."

The android turned and began to walk away; Artim moved over to his father, who had just returned from speaking with the one called Gal'na. To the boy's surprise and delight, Sojef looked at the android and smiled. "Mister Data," he called, and Artim thrilled at the sound of his father addressing the artificial lifeform by name for the first time. "I hope we'll see you again."

Data acknowledged with a pleasant nod as he joined his fellow crew members; grinning, Artim called out:

"Data! Don't forget—you've got to have a little fun every day."

"Good advice," the one called Commander Riker said; he offered his hand to the dark-haired, elegant Troi, who took the proffered hand firmly and smiled up at Riker with a look that made Artim squirm. It was the same look the boy had seen exchanged between adults "in love," and although Father said that in only a few years Artim's attitude would change, at the moment, he found the phenomenon disgusting.

He looked away, toward Captain Picard, who left Anij's side to stand with his officers. The captain pressed a badge on his chest and said: "Picard to *Enterprise* . . . seven to beam up. Energize."

At that instant, Picard gazed over at Anij—and the two of them shared a look that once again forced Artim to look away.

For Anij, the moment before Jean-Luc disappeared in the transporter glow was timeless, as was the memory of him she had impressed on her heart.

It would hurt Sojef to lose her; but he had never had her love to begin with. He had seen her with Picard, and perhaps already knew that she could never wed him now, because her heart belonged—and would, for the rest of her existence—to an offlander.

An offlander who was now gone, for an indefinite period of time: but it mattered not how long he was gone. Anij knew that he would return. For what they had shared had been timeless. Always.

Forever . . .